ARABIC AS A SECRET SONG

CARAF Books

Caribbean and African Literature
Translated from French

Renée Larrier and Mildred Mortimer, Editors

LEÏLA SEBBAR

ARABIC AS A SECRET SONG

Translated by Skyler Artes

Afterword by Mildred Mortimer

UNIVERSITY OF VIRGINIA PRESS

CHARLOTTESVILLE AND LONDON

Originally published in French as *L'arabe comme un chant secret*
Second edition © 2010 by Bleu Autour, Saint-Pourçain-sur-Sioule, France

University of Virginia Press
Translation and afterword © 2015 by the Rector and Visitors
of the University of Virginia
All rights reserved
Printed in the United States of America on acid-free paper

First published 2015

3 5 7 9 8 6 4 2

Library of Congress Cataloging-in-Publication Data
Sebbar, Leïla.
   [Arabe comme un chant secret. English]
   Arabic as a secret song / Leïla Sebbar ; translated by Skyler Artes ;
afterword by Mildred Mortimer.
       pages   cm.—(CARAF books: Caribbean and African literature
translated from French)
   Includes bibliographical references.
   ISBN 978-0-8139-3756-4 (cloth : alk. paper)—ISBN 978-0-8139-3757-1
(pbk. : alk. paper)—ISBN 978-0-8139-3758-8 (e-book)
   1. Sebbar, Leïla. 2. Sebbar, Leïla—Family. 3. Authors, French—20th
century—Biography. 4. Authors, Algerian—20th century—Biography.
5. Algerians—France—Social conditions. I. Artes, Skyler, translator.
II. Title.
   PQ2679.E244Z46 2015
   848'.91403—dc23
   [B]
                                                    2014045922

CONTENTS

ARABIC AS A SECRET SONG

*To all children separated from the language
of their fathers and mothers*

If I Speak My Mother's Language . . .

How did I come back to myself? I didn't ever lose consciousness, not really. I didn't fall to the ground, screaming with my arms flailing about, like they do in novels; I didn't slump over, arms dangling; I didn't hit my head on the side of the bathtub . . . I've never known this way of being away from the world and others. To be mute, yes. Or to disappear into an elsewhere, gaze fixed, body straight and rigid. I was never a run-away. I always left with permission, be it tacit or verbal.

◇◇

I heard someone mention my name. It was my mother. She was talking with some other women, her friends. But me, I wouldn't say anything. I knew when she was talking about me because she would point me out or say my name. If she touched my hair, like mothers do when their child is still small and hasn't yet reached their shoulders, I'd move my head to shake off the weight of her hand. I didn't like this gesture that only came my way when my mother talked with other people about me. Yet I'd stay there. I always heard her say the same thing. I listened anyway. My mother was referring to me when she said: "She's a little skinny," or "She isn't like her sister, who is hardworking, clever, attentive. She never does anything around the house, not even for her dolls. I have to force her. It's terrible . . ." That was me. I'd wait for the rest. And my mother went on: "Always with a book. That's the only thing she likes. What laziness . . ." She'd also say . . . And I knew she was talking about me because she touched my hair.

◇◇

ARABIC AS A SECRET SONG

She walked in front (but I could hear her) with the two women, two sisters whom I found beautiful, without really admitting it to myself. They weren't reserved like my mother. I remember their bodies, hips, breasts; they were soft and large in their blouses and their skirts that were pleated at the waist. I didn't want to see my mother in a bathing suit on the sand. But the women, I'd watch them. I didn't want to see my mother's body. She was thirty. So were the other women. They laughed in the water. My mother? I don't remember. One day, one of the sisters, the youngest one, she showed us little girls how white her skin was where she hadn't tanned. She had a green cotton bathing suit that she had cut out and sewn on the terrace with her sister and my mother. She lowered the triangle of fabric, and I saw her round, white breast and her nipple. I never saw my mother's breasts; she kept herself locked away in the bathroom with my father. I forget whether or not her bathing suit completely covered her breasts. What a sense of surprise and pleasure it was to see this breast, naked but immediately covered up. That feeling. She had no way of knowing it. Her breast had escaped her, it had, in spite of her efforts, slipped out from the top of the bathing suit, and I learned for the first time, lying in the sand, that if I saw women's breasts, I'd be overcome. Whether I realized this in that exact moment, I'm not sure. Yet I now believe that this woman's breast, though I only saw it once, somehow upset me. Her eyes were green and a little sad.

◇◇

All three of them walked in front. They talked. It was the night after the last swim. On the beach, along the sands, on the dirt road. My mother said: "It's the sea. After the sun goes down. A little humidity, some sea spray (I didn't know this word), and her hair gets curly, almost frizzy. She has beautiful hair." The sisters looked at me, saying: "Yes, that's true." One of them touched the frizzy hair around my temples, just above my forehead.

IF I SPEAK MY MOTHER'S LANGUAGE . . .

My mother repeated: "She has beautiful hair. When I do her hair, I like to curl it." I never liked that my mother always said that I had beautiful curly hair; I would have liked straight hair, not curly hair like the little Arab girls I saw in the street had.

◇◇

I came back to myself. From far away. After a very long time. And I put that moment off for a long time. All of these detours. So that I could know that I'm a woman? I'd forgotten the little girl, abandoned in a corner of my history.

◇◇

First, I learned what I wasn't. I wasn't a boy.

I wasn't really Muslim; they would say "Muslims" so as not to say "Arabs," just like later when they said "the events" instead of "the Algerian War," or rather as I heard it said outside of my home. I listened, I rarely spoke. I wasn't French because I had an Arabic name. I didn't know how to answer when girls questioned me. They always asked me the same questions. About my family. I wouldn't say anything. "Does your mother wear the veil? Is your brother circumcised? Does your father eat pork? Does he observe Ramadan?" I'd answer with a yes or a no, as though I were being interrogated. My mother wasn't there to explain who I was. I was mute. I didn't talk with the Arab girls, of whom I saw little, nor did I talk with the other girls, with whom I attended boarding school, the daughters of administrators, colonists, business owners. These girls were gabby and dumb; I despised them yet envied them because they knew who they were: girls from . . . , who lived in . . . , who went to visit . . . , and it was always good, always the best.

◇◇

I slipped away. So as not to answer. Don't say something they'd disapprove of. And don't say what they're expecting me to say.

Who could know me? My father. My mother. Where did I dare to be known? Inside the fence, in the safety of home, with my brother, my sisters, in the yard, in the covered courtyard, in the garden, on the terrace, on the veranda.

◇◇

To someday come all the way back to myself required the detour through books. The political detour. The detour of the war. The detour of women. At last.

Where can I be found? Girl or boy? On the side of the colonized, or of power? Perfect little girl, or rebel?

◇◇

I shouldn't like the French parachutists. They were my father's enemies, and our enemies. When they went past the fence on the other side of the yard, I watched them. In spite of myself. I was troubled. Guilty. They came one day, they took my father, they put him in prison. That was during the war.

◇◇

I learned my father was Arab. But what about me? I spoke my mother's language. My father taught my mother's language to Arab children in the SCHOOL FOR INDIGENOUS BOYS, as the capital letters on the pediment above the entryway indicated. He taught them to read and write in French, the French of schoolbooks:

> A PASSAGE FROM *Bonjour l'École*
> *Lecture et langue française (1st volume)*
>
> é. è. ë.
>
> Hello, Léila!
>
> 1. Here is the teacher! Here is the new student!
>   Hello, new student.
> 2. My name is Léila. Hello, Léila!

IF I SPEAK MY MOTHER'S LANGUAGE . . .

3. You are beautiful, your laugh is pretty, says Dalila.
   Lift your head, Léila, Léila, the student.
4. The student Léila lifts her head and laughs.
   She enters the classroom.*

∞

He was a good teacher, a good father, and an exemplary husband. In my mind. My mother was a strict teacher, a perfect mother, and a perfect wife.

∞

Enclosed in my mother's language, I only heard what came from her, what was conveyed by her, imposed, received, digested, learned, and spit back out. I didn't even want to know that Arabic existed. I didn't speak it. Nor did my mother. She never could. Nor could I. It was the language of my illiterate grandmother, the language of Aïcha and Fatima, also illiterate, and of my father's friends, who used my mother's language to talk with my father and mother. Arabic was the language of the street kids, beyond the fence; they insulted us, the principal's kids. I learned these insults when the boys ran toward us making obscene gestures I barely understood; they were hurled at us from beyond the entryway and while we were on our way to school. I hated them. We walked fast to the French school, the three of us, my sisters and I, holding one another's hands.

My mother's language surrounded me, it still surrounds me. My mother kept me locked away in her language, as though I were still inside her. I locked myself away in books and in the mother tongue—in elementary school, at boarding school, and while studying French literature in France. I learned other languages, but only Latin-based ones.

∞

*The repetition of consonants and vowels in *lève* (lift) and *élève* (student) is lost in English translation.

And what about me, the girl in this story of language and family?

I was my mother's girl, I spoke in her language, I only existed when I told my inquisitors: "My mother is French." "From Metropolitan France," I would add. My roots are where my mother was born, where she had lived. My mother legitimized my Frenchness. "But you, are you French?" "Yes. I looked in the family register. I'm French, I have a French mother." I would repeat: "I'm French, my mother is French." "Is your father French? Why do you have that name? It's not a French name." "I'm also called N.," I would say, giving the very French first name that I'd seen written next to mine on my birth certificate. "But what about your father? Is he French?" I wouldn't answer. "Is he Muslim?" I'd say: "No. He isn't Muslim. He doesn't have a religion." "What about you?" "Me? . . ." "Why is your hair dark and curly like the Arab girls'?" "I don't know." I knew that my father had curly hair like mine. My sisters had my mother's straight hair. "Do you speak Arabic?" "No." "Do you observe Ramadan?" "No." "Do you go to see your father's mom?" "No."

∞

Sometimes we would go to see my grandmother, who lived in Ténès, a village by the sea. She was so small, with piercing eyes. She spoke in Arabic with my father. My mother would sit up straight in her chair and smile the whole time. My father would translate from his mother to his wife, and from his wife to his mother. With ribbons in our hair, white socks and flowered dresses, clean and smiling, we'd sit on the rug at the round table. We'd eat. My father's mother and her daughters, who lived with her, would wrap us up in their arms, kiss us, talk to us . . . We responded by eating. They stuffed us. They told us in their language: "Eat, my girl, eat." My father would translate these words, these words that came to us with every bite, with every one of our pauses, filled again with tenderness and food. They talked to us like mothers, they touched us in a way that my mother never touched us, they fed us with a frenzied, maternal delight. We'd spend the afternoon in the small courtyard, under the fig tree, on mats. My mother always had the right to sit in a chair. My father would take pictures, promising to send them to his mother and sisters, which he always did. And we'd leave. Without having seen the sea.

"Do you know your father's mother? Do you to go to see her?" "No."

I didn't often see my father's mother. I know my father loved her. She raised five children on her own. She sacrificed her two daughters to impotent or alcoholic husbands and raised her sons for colonial society. Two of them. Kader stayed in Ténès, ever true to Koranic law, to his mother, and to his sisters. She died three years ago, maybe, I don't really know exactly when; my father never talked about it. My father's a man who doesn't talk much. He waits for others to talk. He listens. He's the Patient One, that's what his name means. But if it's written in French letters, does he recognize his name? I never knew anything but this name, written in the way that the French administration wrote it on identification papers, on my father's papers, and on mine, where I carry my father's name. Whenever I heard my father's name uttered by an Arab, I couldn't tell that it was my name too. But when a French person said it, the name immediately took on a French sound with which I identified. I could recognize myself with this particular name. Anytime I had to state my name, I had to spell it, repeating it several times. I always anticipated someone saying: "What kind of name is that?" or "That's not a French name." "It's my name," I'd say, and they'd leave me alone. One day, someone, a Frenchwoman, told me: "You have a beautiful name. It's beautiful, Leïla Sebbar." That was the war. The boarding school protected us girls from attacks.

ARABIC AS A SECRET SONG

∞

My father had returned from prison. He never talked about it. I only saw, in the back of a drawer in the mirrored armoire, in their room, a pile of letters that my mother had received from my father when he was in prison. I never read them. One day I will. I'm reluctant to say when.

∞

I knew that my father was Arab. I knew that I was Arab too, because of my father. The woman who told me that I had a beautiful name, I loved her for that, and also because she spoke my mother's language, without the accent of the Frenchwomen from here. A language that, for me, hadn't been contaminated by the colonial language; it was a clear and pure language. For me. Back then.

∞

She had green eyes. I loved listening to her talk. This woman came from France, like my mother. She was born there. She spoke the same language. She was a woman, like my mother, but younger. She couldn't have been my mother. She was younger than my mother was when she walked along the shore with the two sisters, her friends, and talked about me. My mother's friends, those who walked next to her along the sea, spoke her language. I knew that they were foreigners. I knew it because of their laughter and their bodies, which were ample, full, supple, and their gestures; they didn't have my mother's stiffness, they had big thighs where children could sit. As they spoke, we were behind them or at their sides, running. If I heard my name, I'd listen to them while they talked about me.

She told me that my name was beautiful, and so I heard it and recognized it. It was my name, my father's name, an Arab name, the one in front of my first name that, at my birth, announced that I was a girl, an Arab man's daughter. This first name that they had picked for me, that I state when I am asked, "What is your name," that I hear when someone calls me, I know that it's me. When I hear it, I feel overwhelmed, as though saying my name meant telling me "I love you."

◇◇

Often, when someone calls to me, I'm not called by name. So as not to touch the essential lyricism of my first name, no one says it. A gesture, a wave of the hand, or an inarticulate yell: "Hey! Hey!" or "Say . . ." Or if people are talking near me, they talk to me without using my name. The voices that do say it, I can hear them and I'm always moved by this sort of echoing of my name. Where is it inscribed, or marked within me, this first name that resonates so? This feminine first name. Not from here. I say while laughing: "Woman of the sands, woman of the Plateaus. Arab of the desert and the sea."

◇◇

Sometimes I want to free my first name from the last, from the name itself. And when I hear it, it's as though I hear my name and not the one that is in front and next to it. It's there, said and spoken, when my mother said, as she so often did: "Leïla doesn't like housework." My mother also called me to come inside, for housework or homework. Never for love; I don't remember hearing my name called out in a loving way, or perhaps I've forgotten.

When my mother said my name, it was, more often than not, a reprimand; it was said in anger, it was a call to order, it was the sound of disappointment. My teacher of a mother, manager of the house. Perhaps she said my name tenderly when I was sick, as though I were going to die—I don't remember. If I'd fainted in the house, she would have said my name, she would have said my name over and over, worried and desperate for me to hear her. Finally, overcome and loving. I wouldn't have heard her. I never fainted.

My mother still says my name. Just like before. At home, during my childhood. "Leïla." The only word that escaped from my mother's language. The only one that I still hear and that creates a sort of scandal, lost there, present on a page or in someone's voice. The only one that proves to this day that my mother's tongue wounded me, just as it did my father.

◇◇

It's by way of this name, this name of mine, that I searched for Adonis, *le bon nègre,* in old forgotten books, in the catalogues of the National Library, in Paris.* I didn't know what I would find in Adonis, that black slave, or in all of the African slaves of eighteenth-century colonial tales. They learned to speak the French master's language, and the master told them that they were good slaves. Some of them became school principals and French teachers.

My name is Leïla and I teach my mother's language to those who speak it because they speak their mother's language. And I write in my mother's language. To return to myself. I was a good colonial subject. Like my father. I wasn't a girl.

◇◇

Paris. Books. Political meetings. May '68. Action committees. Neighborhood committees. Vietnam. Emigrants. The working class.

Who called me by name? I'd hear my name when in love and know that I was a woman. But, for me, people put love next to politics and demonstrations. Because of the potential for chaos.

---

*See J. B. Piquenard, *Adonis ou le bon nègre* (Paris: Didot, 1798), a text Sebbar examines in her thesis, "Le mythe du bon nègre ou l'idéologie coloniale dans la production romanesque du XVIIIe siècle."

I didn't speak in meetings. I spoke in private. In a loving embrace. Where did I exist? Where was I a woman? Who knew my name? Activists must forget their names. I fought anonymously. *SNP,* just like the colonial administration called those whom it hadn't registered and those whose ethnicity it refused, the unpronounceable, unhearable, undecipherable Arab name. *SNP: Sans nom patronymique,* without family name. I had no name.

I'd even invented a secret name, as everyone else had. In '68 we thought that if the police registered these names, we'd avoid inquiries . . . So I took on an alias and kept my name well hidden. Seven years later, a woman whom I'd met during this time of my life called me by this false name. I'd forgotten it. It was a name with French roots; it could have been that of my mother's mother, a woman from Périgord.

◇◇

The Women's Liberation Movement. I learned that my name is Leïla. I spoke. About myself. I'd forgotten everything. I believed . . . Alongside other women, I searched for myself, the little girl, on the banks of a woman's childhood. To know. I came back to myself. The road was long. It's difficult. Still. This history I have with women.

If I sign my name at the bottom of what I write, I'm rid of it, so that I never hear it again. Yet if I don't write it, I'm lost.

If I Do Not Speak My Father's Language . . .

At home on the colonial school grounds where we lived, I used to hear a language that wasn't my mother's. Our wash was done in the back of the garden, just beyond the grape arbor, near the wicker swing (or was it simply a plank of smooth wood?) that my father had set up in the shade of the medlar tree. The woman who did our wash worked in the laundry room, which was surrounded by lilac bushes and giant deep purple mallows—even after learning a few words of my mother's language, she always said "lindry room," stressing this "i" sound in spite of my mother's corrections. My mother, the Roumia, the Frenchwoman from France. For the laundrywoman who came to the principal's house every day, my father would translate the daily chores into Arabic. Their exchange was brief, routine, and lingered as a sort of ritual exchange even when the woman was able to understand the French teacher's language. My father's voice changed for this woman; it sounded more fluid, even for the domestic demands and necessities he brought to the attention of my mother, who never spent the morning in the house but instead on the other side of the door to the veranda that opened onto the large covered courtyard in front of the schoolyard, which stretched out to the left and to the right all the way to the fence and the classrooms. My mother taught French to more than forty Arab boys; she had a strong commitment to her vocation, one that the Algerian War would disrupt. For the time being, she was sure that what she was doing was right, all the more so with the young, native teacher, whom she followed at the age of twenty onto the high plateaus; he was just starting as a principal, freshly out of the Bouzaréa Teachers College in Algiers, working as the principal of this SCHOOL FOR INDIGENOUS BOYS; that's what's written in uppercase letters above the porch next to the house. After thirty years I don't know if those carved letters are still fixed in stone or if certain letters have disappeared or if someone chipped away the "INDIGENOUS" and preserved the "SCHOOL FOR BOYS" after Algeria's independence, or if everything has disappeared from the pediment. I haven't returned to this village school, to my father's school, where I wasn't a student.

◇◇

Each morning, my two young sisters and I would walk to the girls' school in the European neighborhood. We crossed the hardened dirt esplanade where the boys from the Arab neighborhood played ball as soon as their mothers where done drying the red peppers they would later grind with a copper mortar and pestle—we could hear the sound all the way from school. Before entering the courtyard, the boys would shout foreign Arabic words at us, the principal's daughters. Words from the street and from their mother's language, they were insults, words we could understand because they were more aggressive. Some would stop their game and join together to call us names from a distance. We'd walk fast, holding one another's hands, all the way to the grassy hill we had to climb. The boys wouldn't follow us, but we'd still hear them yelling among themselves; they'd forgotten us.

◇◇

I recognized my father's language in the language of those Arab boys, who would roll down the gently sloping road, past the windows of our room, on boards strapped together to make wagons of sorts, rolling toward the old train station, which had fallen into disuse. Forgetting that he, like them, had been a child of the streets, maybe he too had insulted French girls—but he never told me about it, and I never asked him questions about his boyhood secrets in the Arab neighborhoods of Ténès, his birthplace—I didn't hear the same language when my father spoke with the laundrywoman. Yet they'd speak this language together. The woman didn't limit her replies to a simple "yes" in Arabic as she did with my mother, my mother who, as soon as the woman seemed to understand, believed that the woman had, by some miracle, understood everything. Did they only talk about the chores that needed to be done in the morning while my mother was out? Sometimes they'd start laughing in Arabic without my knowing why, but I heard that foreign and familiar laugh as an invitation to share in this joyous language, the very language of those boys I feared on the road to the girls' school. When those boys were free from the colonial school, they no longer spoke the language of the classroom; they shouted, as they shouted when they raced together through the big double-door gates in the courtyard just after the teacher rang the school bell. They ran in every direction. The violent clamor crashed into the veranda door, the door we didn't dare open, fearing they might rush in and trample us; we'd leave through the school gate just below, smelling the grape must from the cooperative wine cellar that faced the garden.

◇◇

In front of my father's desk, in the gloomy vestibule that opened onto the row of classrooms, women waited as though for an appointment at the clinic. They cried or laughed, spoke among themselves in my father's language, the one he used with the laundrywoman: the intonations were the same; the interjections and the gestures gave the general meaning of their conversations. Again, when I hear these women speak I hear my father's language, a language I don't understand; I catch some words, the general outline of the spoken language. Without disturbing the women, I stay there to listen. One day my father let me secretly stay with him, though I wasn't hiding, in the principal's office, where the women would come to talk about their sons.

◇◇

It's nearly summer. The window is open; it's already hot. The narrow garden, full of orange trees, borders the office and classrooms. It ends at the front gate, closed by the fence above the low perimeter wall. Wild roses grow on the trellis. My father put some beehives in the shade of the orange trees. We often saw him, in his hat and bee mask, his hands gloved, taking care of the bees. He likes saying that he learned beekeeping at the school in Bouzaréa. As for the asparagus that he grows with the bigger kids in the kitchen garden in front of the school, he says the same thing: he learned this at "Bouzaréa"; he says this all the time.

◇◇

The women don't remove their veils when they sit down on the other side of the desk. With their veil still on, they uncover their faces. Sometimes they come in two at a time, sisters, or a mother and a daughter, or a grandmother and a mother, or maternal aunts. They all wear bracelets that jingle as they move their hands. They use their hands a lot when they talk, and they talk endlessly. My father lets them talk as long as they want. If a bee enters the room, they aren't afraid. My father says in Arabic that his bees aren't bad, the women agree and they shoo the bees away with the back of their hands, their palms and fingertips dyed red with henna. Some are tattooed, others aren't. Their eyes are darkened with *khôl*; their hair is hidden under the scarves knotted at their temples.

◇◇

My father forgot that I was there. I stay still. I listen. The women pretend not to see me. Some of them come from far away; they want to leave with a signed paper. If they return empty-handed, their day would've been wasted. I don't know what my father writes on those papers that he signs below his stamp; the women look at their paper for a long while before carefully folding it up and placing it into a small purse that they had taken out of their *saroual* when they arrived at the office. During these afternoon hours, I recognize my father's voice in the language he speaks with the laundrywoman who works at the end of the alleyway planted with blue iris. My mother takes care of our kitchen garden and the flower garden. The native principal's language is calm and lilting, firm, yet with none of the coarseness of those street boys. He speaks the language of the illiterate women who come by foot, by cart, or by bus to get their papers signed in the principal's office. I don't know how many times my father has opened and closed the narrow, vertical cabinet with the wooden runners where he keeps his papers. I love the delicate sound of this door that opens from top to bottom. When the women stop talking, they, like me, follow my father's movements: the glass-paned cabinets, the desk drawers, the paper, the fountain pen and ink, the blotter, the stamp; and then, when he writes, they pay careful atten-tion, their hands folded, concealing the flowers printed on their dresses, flowers their veils don't hide. My father gets up and moves to that open window. The screen needs to be replaced; it was so rusted that we wound up removing it. He speaks in Arabic as he stands in front of the orange trees and wild roses. Perhaps the women said that the scent of the roses pleases the bees just as much as it pleases them. Perhaps they talked about the honey the men collect in the colonists' orchards where they work. I now understand the exchange of formulaic greetings when my father and the women nod to one another. Speaking first, my father asks each woman in turn about her and her children's health before he himself sits down. Once, he kissed a very old woman on her scarf-covered forehead; she'd accompanied her daughter-in-law. She didn't talk; it was the young woman who expressively explained her problem. From the open window, my father tells this last arrival that if she wants to avoid the storm, she could take shelter on the veranda. The woman expresses her gratitude, they exchange more customary phrases, and then she leaves. My father closes the wooden shutters, he hesitates, he leaves the windows open; the shutters are still watertight, though they need to be cleaned and repainted. He says: "The storm's almost here. Quickly, get the laundry." I run toward the house.

◇◇

At the back of the garden, in front of the laundry room, my mother and the laundrywoman move quickly. We hear the thunder. Large raindrops fall on the hardened dirt. My mother throws the laundry into a wicker basket. It's not too hot out, but the garden smells like it does at the end of a summer day when the falling rain raises wet splatters of dusty dirt. Everyone is yelling—my sisters, my father, me, my mother, and her helper. My father picks up the basket and runs to the veranda. The cats have found refuge under the lemon tree next to the kitchen. My father talks to the laundrywoman, saying she should get home because her mother's waiting for her. My mother isn't listening; she's already folding the dry laundry on the large table in front of the glass door. The storm continues. We play with our baby dolls, dressing them in warm clothes—jackets and woolen knickers that my mother showed my sisters and me how to knit. The laundrywoman puts on the *haïk* she had left in the room by the kitchen, then says "good-bye everyone" in French, without my mother correcting her; she tries hard. My father takes out his new car and drives the woman back to her mother's house; it's the first time she's ridden in the passenger seat. She laughs, covering her face. Away from the rain, under the porch, where you can read "SCHOOL FOR INDIGENOUS BOYS," the children watch the departure of the latest model, a black Peugeot 202 that my father bought a few days ago. It's shiny and clean, it has a black luggage rack, silver chrome wings, a black grill covering the headlights. Twice the woman catches her veil in the car door; she laughs and says in Arabic that she's a bit of a ninny. The car leaves under the sounds of shouts, bravos, and thunder.

◇◇

A storm hit just as suddenly to the west of Oran toward the end of an afternoon as we were sitting under the olive trees eating lamb during the celebration of Eid. It nearly ruined the feast. My father and the other village men and boys had been busy since dawn preparing the two sheep for the festival. His friend, who was the head of the small village school for boys, spent one week fattening up the two sheep he kept in an olive grove. How is it that I can clearly remember the village's name, Le Khémis, and my father's friend's name, Khelladi? He had sons: Mourad must have been the same age as me. His wife didn't sit with us at the high table in the dining room at our home on the school grounds. I found the trip to Le Khémis in the Peugeot 202 to be long and dry. There were bare hills like the Agriates in Corsica, but without the cactus that surrounded the flat houses. It's very early in the morning. Everyone's sleeping, except for the men and my father and the boys who were helping to prepare the pit to grill the lamb. I was there, hidden by the centenary trunk of an olive tree. I was up before everyone else, just as I was when I wanted to eat the ripe figs in the kitchen garden before everyone else. My father speaks with the men and boys in Arabic.

◇◇

He doesn't seem to be giving orders, but he isn't speaking like he does with the women who come to his office or with the laundrywoman or with the women in his family, his mother and older sisters, whom we visit regularly in the Arab town of Ténès, "old Ténès," where they live in the house in which they were born; his mother brought her five children into the world while standing upright in the middle of a circle of women. And so her sons were born to a mother who stood up; my father always said proudly that this was an honor. She held on to a rope attached to the ceiling, and she bit down on it so that she wouldn't scream too loudly. She had to give birth standing upright. My father brought us to see his mother and his sisters in the old house where they all lived together. He spoke his mother's language with them, forgetting the other language, the language of the school and his wife. They were so talkative; they would talk with my mother as if she could understand. My mother would listen, nod, and smile. They'd touch her in an effort to communicate better; they thought she was beautiful, just as they thought we were beautiful, we, the children of this foreign woman and the son of the house, the loyal and generous oldest child, the favorite son, the beloved brother. They mustn't have thought that he had betrayed them by marrying the Frenchwoman. Their gestures proved the opposite. They'd hold my mother's hands, they'd look at her, they'd admire her, never ceasing to speak, their Arabic embracing her like a child, just as Arabic embraced us while we ate at the low table. They'd feed us with this tireless language and traditional dishes that they'd prepared for us long in advance of our arrival. My father's mother, short and intense, dressed in her *saroual* and delicately flowered shirt, the same shirt that her taller and heavier daughters wore. She'd talk endlessly in the piercing voice of a curious old woman; the sound of her voice was softened by the thick and tender voices of her pale-eyed daughters, one of whom was nearly blind. My grandmother would also communicate with her small black eyes, which were just as lively as her tongue.

◇◇

My father's language is rougher with the men who tend the sheep. The boys speak among themselves, but others, far beyond the wall, shout like the boys on the path to the girls' school. Was it my father who slit the animal's throat, or was it one of the other men? I don't really know if it was my father; maybe he was dressed like the other men, in an old *djellabah,* to protect his work clothes. He isn't wearing his grey teacher's jacket that I always saw him wearing on school days. Was it my father in a *djellabah,* or another Arab? My father never wore what the men in the countryside wore, not the baggy pants, nor the vest, nor the turban, though I saw a picture of him at Bouzaréa Teachers College: he was wearing a *chéchia,* but it must have been part of a uniform, or else it was simply a vestige of a different time in his life. I don't know if the man is wearing straight or baggy pants under the *djellabah.* The sheep is bound, the man holds a long, sharp knife, he leans toward the sheep's head; he holds it from behind—he has the help of the boys who talk loudly to one another—and with one stroke he slits the animal's throat. Perhaps he's the village butcher; I don't think it's my father. The men speak in Arabic over the bleeding sheep, whose legs kick for a few seconds more while held down by the laughing boys. The boys continue to talk loudly while moving the slaughtered sheep to the olive tree, where my father hangs it up so that it can be skinned and gutted. Blood runs from its gaping throat. The flopping head stains one of the boys' *gandourah;* he mimics the yelling he'll hear from his mother when he arrives home with a bloodstained *gandourah.* He was circumcised a long time ago: he wore that white *gandourah* for many days; it was bloody and glorious. He doesn't wear it anymore; it'll be passed down to his younger brothers. He fights with the other boy, accusing him of getting his *gandourah* dirty; they yell at each other in Arabic. The men yell back, demanding silence, but then they make the boys leave because they continued to shout. The man with the knife cuts off the sheep's head. It'll be grilled separately with the brain. The men, who have been on their feet since dawn, will eat it quietly. The guests, who are French for the most part, don't know that the head is the best part. My father skins the sheep with the long knife. There's no more blood. He talks with the men who are preparing the fire; the way they talk is calm and serene, like the way they handle the kindling. They don't talk the whole time. In nearly regular intervals, someone speaks and then stops, and the others answer. They work silently for a while. My father cuts the sheep open; the innards make a wet thump as they fall into the metal pail we call "the can." The boys have returned; stray dogs have jumped over the wall, the boys chase them with sticks. One dog knocks over the can, the men make threats, and the boys run off with the dogs. The boys come back later to relieve the men, who must turn the spit for hours on end. They put the sheep on the spit and place the long stick on two big rocks above the red coals lying at the bottom of the pit. The men squat around the glistening, clean sheep my father so carefully prepared. Their easy conversation follows. My father prepares the liver skewers, square chunks of liver wrapped in a thin veil of fat. He grills a few pieces for the men. I move toward them. My father sees me for the first time this morning. He says: "So, you were hiding here? For how long? Come, have a taste." He talks to the men in Arabic: he talks about me, they laugh, my father laughs, too, he runs his hand through my hair. I squat at the edge of the pit next to a man with baggy striped pants, rolled up shirtsleeves, his turban loose at the nape of his neck. My father checks the first skewer—the best, he said in Arabic, and then in French, the choicest piece. He shares it. One of the men divides a flatbread. We eat in silence. At the foot of one of the olive trees, my father pulls violet figs, covered in large green leaves, from a big basket, a fig for everyone. The men thank him in Arabic. And me, I eat while squatting next to the man who is holding one end of the long stick he must turn regularly.

My father returns from the field with a water jug wrapped in a wet cloth. He unwraps it. I raise the jug, tip my head back, and let the water flow into my mouth, just like my father taught us, and then the men do the same. For the rest of the day, my father doesn't speak in his language.

◇◇

I walk through the village streets with my sisters; we go toward the fountain where the donkeys and horses drink. Gangs of boys are yelling all around us, just like the boys on the path to school. They make fun of our curls, of the plaid ribbons in our hair, of our white bobby socks, of our pleated plaid skirts that come just above the knee and are held up with suspenders. They have the other girls witness this. The boys laugh and shout words at us that make their sisters feel ashamed; these girls hide their faces in the crooks of one another's necks as they giggle. Toward the end of the afternoon, before the storm, protected by the French people from the school, I go down to the river and grottos with my sisters. The boys are gone.

◇◇

At the spot where the river forms an irregular and calm lake, on the flat stones, women wash clothes, their legs bare, their *sarouals* and skirts lifted. They aren't veiled, but scarves cover their hair. Little girls run through the water; their hair, rolled in thick cotton ribbons of yellow and red, is pulled into ponytails that fall down their back. They talk to one another and the women, they don't work with their mothers yet, they take care of the littlest kids while the women beat the clothes and help one another wring out the heavier pieces—often woolen ones— which they stretch out over the shrubs on the edge of the river. They speak loudly, they yell, they laugh like the laundrywoman does when her sister comes to our house at school to help her with spring cleaning: the blankets, the winter clothes, the bedspreads that must be washed. I'm alone, lost in this secret bend in the river. The Arab voices of these women cover the voices of the teachers, the men and women who are calling the children in from the storm. The women haven't seen me. I watch them, I listen to them. I'll leave when they leave. I'll walk in the sounds of their language and laundry all the way to the village, where my father is looking for me. My father says nothing to me. The oldest women speak to him in his language. Are they protecting me? My father thanks them and bids them farewell before turning toward the school. We hear the thunder, the sky is black over the house, my father walks fast, I hold his hand. In the severe language of the school, he says: "We were afraid because of the river." "I was with the women." "I know." A hard, thick rain begins to fall. My father squeezes my hand. We run toward the school playground.

I forgot to mention that my father's eyes are blue.

My Father's Body in My Mother's Language

What are ancestors, exactly? Is it enough to do a genealogy? An illiterate, reclusive, devout Muslim for a paternal grandmother and a poacher, peasant, radical-socialist for a maternal grandfather? I see my grandfather as a peasant. Later, I'll find out that he was a policeman. If he'd been alive during the conquest of Algeria, he would've been a farmer-soldier taking orders from Bugeaud, who was also a rural Périgordian. But would he have burned the orchards and the wheat and barley fields, would he have obeyed the general's military strategy? I'd like to think that he wouldn't have.

∞

My grandmother's alive. I see her when I go to visit; she looks at me with her small black eyes the same way that she looks at my mother, the Frenchwoman. She speaks in Arabic with her son, the Frenchwoman's husband. I don't know what she tells him. I'll never know what she thinks when she looks at me like that, when I feel her inquisitive eyes upon me. In the inner courtyard, under the fig tree, my mother sits on a chair. She listens to my father as he translates his mother's words, though I've forgotten which words. I'm not quite sure that this small woman is anything at all to me. If she is, then by what accident of nature? She speaks with her daughters, my father's sisters, in my father's language. To us children, the sisters speak the universal female language of the nursery. These words don't belong to any particular language; the words are simply the sounds that accompany their caring, familial gestures as they feed us, the oldest son's children, the son who sends money to the lonely widows living in his childhood home, the son who crossed the sea only to return with a foreign woman, his wife, the mother of the children sitting around the low table and reveling in the discovery of this exotic food.

∞

My grandfather, in the peasant's house right near a beautiful and peaceful part of the Dronne River. A small green and blue boat on its banks. As a child, my mother went out with her father to fish for trout with her bare hands. I don't know if my grandfather sees us. The rules are strict. Obedience, manners, frugality. We walk silently next to the wheelbarrow he pushes to the tobacco field or to a corner of the vineyard. My father speaks with him in my grandfather's language. I don't remember if he ever talked with me. I've forgotten his voice. We play under the wooden planks of the old cart in the shed. We spend hours in the heat, the aromas drifting in from the baker's oven next door. I know, or I learned much later, that his adopted daughter is Eurasian. Is she his adopted daughter or his real daughter? He must have been involved with the war in Indochina, and maybe—since nobody has seen a Vietnamese woman in the village—he had to leave his concubine, his *con-gaï,* back in Indochina just like Michel Ragon's father, whose son discovered the letters from Asia and his half-sister *aux yeux d'Asie,* with Asia's eyes. I don't know what my relationship is to this rough man, my mother's father. It takes days and days of travel to visit him in his French village. It takes a few hours in the roomy black Peugeot 202 to visit my grandmother in Ténès.

∞

How many lives, how many books, how many words would I need to believe that these are my ancestors? I needed the war, the Algerian War, to be struck with that thunderous certainty that I'm the daughter of an Arab man and a French woman, that France colonized Algeria, that my father is colonized and my mother is the colonizer (colonizeress?), that I'm divided in spite of the words that are supposed to reassure me: that my father and mother belong to the same political family . . . A political family—what does that matter when family origins, the father's side and the mother's side, are left out of everyday conversation? All points of reference are amnesiac.

◇◇

Silence covers my mother's Catholic traditions; silence covers my father's Muslim and Algerian traditions. The rule-bound secular republic is the center. It's honored, ideal, absolute in every act, in every word. The sacred place. My father, the indigenous teacher of the French language in the school belonging to France, principal of the SCHOOL FOR INDIGENOUS BOYS. His school is the singular, beloved cradle of the secular, republican speech that is endlessly and passionately recited in the schools. My mother is the mission's unwavering ally, a teacher in the school that my father runs, school mistress and mistress of the house that is attached to this minuscule, secular republic. My father, the undisputed master of this ideal island, would be a poor colonized man, a victim, and my mother, his accomplice in the school, the house, the bedroom, would be the executioner, the executioneress? It's impossible to feminize this barbarous word. And so my father's school is the colonial school. It's the school of colonial and colonialist France. It colonized my father in my mother's language. It was an abduction. My father was stolen from his mother, from his land, from his country—since he was a part of an internationalist political network—from his language, and from the women who spoke his language. He chose Satan. He lost his soul . . . And my mother is the diabolical seductress, the auxiliary of an imperial and warmongering France.

◇◇

Where am I in this history of body, souls, and language? Daughter of a victim and of an executioneress. Trapped. Tormented. Between a feminized masculine and a masculinized feminine. Who is the father, and who is the mother? A neuter result, neither daughter nor son, child of an unnatural union. Flee to the geography of the body and mind so that I might escape the madness. Flee. Find refuge far away, on the other side of the sea. In exile. In the silence of libraries and in other peoples' books. Seclusion, without the protection of a family, because a genealogy doesn't speak. Deprived of a native land, of memory, of a father and mother, of the wholeness of the female body, domestic, earthly, separated from my father's language, a language that was never spoken—my mother's language draws me closer yet. I'm among the books in my mother's language, in the library's labyrinth; I'm forever within the institutional symbol of this written language. Surrounded, corseted. Outside, I bear an insect's armor; inside, I've disintegrated. Just like my father, an intimate and familiar foreigner. And so, renouncing the deathly safety of shadows and of books, with my lone, mute body wandering from one periphery to the next, I stop near the sound of that spoken, emotional language. Arab women converse in a sad square on French soil. I walk again and again, alone, through the displaced words, through the voices of women who speak in exile. In this world of concrete, in this new land where I write my father's body in my mother's language, France's language, in my agitated, violent, and reserved language, I'm followed and seduced by the voice, the voices of Arab women who will not stay silent. Woman of a sabotaged patio, of a tribe that never existed. Desperate archaeologist, confident in this pursuit of disparate fragments, but fragments for which impossible body? Does Isis, my mother's language, resuscitate the body of Algeria, my father?

*The Mothers of My Father's People
in My Mother's Language*

The women sit in a circle. At first you cannot see where, except that they aren't in the courtyard of a Moorish house, nor on the hardened dirt in the shade of the cactus encircling the village. If you look carefully, mounds of dirt appear between the women, who are huddled closely together, speaking quietly around a tomb. The white veils fill with invisible wind, they turn their backs on the indiscreet photographic eye. Nothing more than these three or four women surrounding the gently disturbed red dirt, forming a curve, from head to foot. I'm not sure that they're talking to one another. I watch them for a moment.

◇◇

Agnès Varda invited me, along with some other writers, to say a few words about a black-and-white photo. It was a job for television or film—I don't remember which. I talk about what I see in the photo; I forget what I was able to say, but I haven't forgotten my tears. I don't know why, but I began to cry; even to this day I wonder, and it's not that I want to stop these tears that were sudden and irrepressible in front of a photograph that was so simple and so meagerly tragic. There's no immediate reason, nothing apparent. Agnès Varda stops her work and calmly waits for the tears to stop. She says to me: "You'd like to have had an Arab mother?" The surprise of this comment prevents me from responding; uneasiness too. What right did this woman, whom I didn't know, have to ask such a question? A question that I hear as an affirmation, and also, in some way, as being an offense toward my mother, my French mother. A hasty and misplaced assumption that wasn't necessary. In truth, I'd never wished for a different mother; I say this in good conscience. How many years later—I'm not able to recall the date of this afternoon, on rue Daguerre, in Agnès Varda's house—the scene of the women comes back to me, and my tears. Reflecting on the fictional mother in my books, I think back on the film director's question, on her insight. I'm not the mother in my books, my mother isn't the mother in my books; the mother in my books is obstinately an Arab, Muslim woman, an Algerian.

◇◇

My mother. She is France. I know this; I have always known this. She is the language of France. She doesn't say it, but everything proves it—her gestures, her bearing, her voice. In the working-class Arab neighborhood, which we don't refer to as the *"village nègre"* (though they do in Oran, in Sidi Bel-Abbès . . .), in this neighborhood on the outskirts of town, far from the European houses and the colonial center where my father, the indigenous teacher, runs the school for indigenous boys, my mother is unique. No other woman looks like her. The teacher, the Frenchwoman from France, speaks the language of the Republic's school, the language of books and of France, in the way that all French people beyond the Mediterranean should speak it, in the country where, from Marseilles to Lille, they speak the language of Paris. And Paris is France. I'm sure of this even when I walk in the forests of chestnut trees in my mother's land, in Dordogne.

◇◇

The wife of the indigenous teacher, the beautiful foreigner, the Frenchwoman who is not afraid of Arabs, she doesn't understand that those who are born in this country—from father to son and from mother to daughter, they're so close to the indigenous people who are at home here on their own land, just as they have been since long before the latest conquerors arrived—act as if they're in danger whenever groups of men or gangs of youths pass by, speaking their primitive language. This woman, who doesn't shy away from the poor people of the countryside and the large colonial farms, speaks another language. They find her strange and different, they find her voice to be like a fresh spring; the words are the same, but the sounds are different—less rushed, less forced, less filled with air. They listen to her in the school garden, in the courtyard and on the red path by the wine cellar. This language isn't the Colony's language. It's beautiful.

◇◇

My mother teaches barefoot boys and peasant children, who come from afar, the proper language, the correct accent—the pronunciation must be perfect. With us, her children, she speaks her language, and just as at school, she corrects the faulty words and the wrong sounds that slip out, furtively, when we speak. My mother, the teacher. Words and gestures are under surveillance. Always. The Colony's language didn't cross the threshold to the school and our home. Not that language, nor the overly bright colors of the women born in this land of heat and prosperity, nor their shiny jewelry, nor their showy accessories. They tell me that my mother is beautiful, elegant, and modern. She flips through fashion magazines while sitting in the patio chair on the veranda. Later, in the other country, I thought I saw that chair, displayed alongside other objects taken from abandoned homes, I thought it was the same one, the chair from the terrace where we had our ritual coffee. I move closer: the wood is too light, the wicker isn't the same color; I turn away. My mother sits, she wears her dress with blue irises, she turns the pages of the fashion magazine, attentive to the style that appeals to her; she will choose one out of several styles to make with the seamstress who comes to the house on Thursdays. She's a Jew from Tlemcen, she is bosomy, in a fitted sunflower yellow suit that my mother must've found to be too yellow. Though she never said so, I know she would've thought so, though I'm sure to this day that if I ask her the color of the seamstress's suit, she'll say that she doesn't remember. My mother chooses fancy clothes for us, her daughters, my two sisters and me. For herself she chooses dresses and suits whose fabric, of the highest quality, is the only ornament. Maybe a lapel in a sober, white piqué, or a slightly dulled silver broach. Refined patterns and colors for her and for us, the Frenchwoman's daughters. The teacher. To learn the simple, essential, daily ways of order, cleanliness, harmony. We'll know how to do everything perfectly at home and at school. The vigilant, attentive eye of this mistress of the house and school. Read, write, sew, knit, cook, garden, arrange flowers, be beautiful, obedient, orderly, studious, helpful, capable, perfect, the model daughter of a model mother. My father's proud of his wife and daughters.

◇◇

Our home on the school grounds, my mother's garden, and her children form a little France where France's language is spoken. The servants, Aïcha and Fatima, with their white veils, the *haïk,* lifted, folded up, and put away in the house, work hard to follow the gestures that educate them and the words they learn to pronounce perfectly; my tireless mother corrects them. My father says that Aïcha is a lioness. I understand that Aïcha protects herself like a lion, I understand that she learns quickly; Aïcha is a good student, my mother's best student. When the day comes for her to leave and get married, and for her younger sister Fatima to replace her, my mother says: "Aïcha was a lioness." In the first text I wrote on Algerian childhood, I recall Aïcha and Fatima. Aïcha, on a laundry day, at the back of my mother's garden, next to the steaming washtub; I sit on a brick, the tall stems of oxblood red hollyhocks behind me. In that moment, when I leave the words of the university and the body of that language of school, books, and libraries, the voices of the other language return, the gestures of humble, domestic, and illiterate bodies. My mother used to say: "If Aïcha had gone to school . . ." Whenever my father repeats "Aïcha is a lioness," I think I understand that she's smart, exceptionally so. It was as if he were using her as an example for us. Aïcha didn't go to school, and yet . . . If she had gone to school . . . I'm not sure what would've happened next. Later, I tell myself that she would have been a nurse in the *maquis,* just like the girls who joined their brothers in completing elementary or middle school. In prison, her illiterate sisters, along with other women, learned their father's language and the enemy's language. They met improvised teachers, worried about their future in an independent Algeria. What happens next . . .

◇◇

And so Aïcha becomes, in spite of me, the mother in my books. I write about her body and her language in my mother's language, the language of France, which she will never know how to read or write. I didn't go into the two sisters' house. They live in the Arab village not far from the school. I don't know where their father's house is, or if they have a father or a mother. I know nothing about them. I see them in the morning and at night, dressed as Arab women—veiled, unveiled, they have dresses with large flowers. I can just make out a strand of hair near the ear there where the scarf slipped. They tie and retie the scarf or scarves above their forehead; the flattened strands of hair on their temples mustn't show. Slowly and precisely, they adjust the striking colors that hide their hair. Because their palms are red, I know that they dye their hair with henna. How? I've heard it said, though I've never attended a henna ceremony; I don't go to the Moorish bath. There is a bathroom with a shower at our house. My mother would never go to a Moorish bath. Everything separates her from the women of my father's people.

◇◇

Everything separates me from my father's mother and sisters. Language, gestures, manners, domestic norms. We must sit on cushions around a low table, we must eat everything that is served, be respectful. The old aunts talk to us about unfamiliar dishes cooked at length, about bread baked at home, about honey and almond cakes for us, the children of the favorite son. We must eat and say it's good. We eat and we eat; the old sisters—they weren't really old—watch us without eating, touched, astonished by our skirts, which they find to be too short, by the plaid ribbons in our hair, by our very white canvas sandals, by the way we chatter in an unfamiliar language. They're heavy, they wear flowered blouses, baggy pants, their carrot-red hair escaping from their layered scarves. My father's sisters. And so, my father has a mother and sisters who seem as old as his mother; they look like Aïcha and Fatima will look when they're no longer young. They take us into their arms, squeezing us against their soft blouses, hugging us while laughing; they mispronounce my brother's and sisters' French names. Even though we're so different, they're happy with us, sitting under the jasmine in the courtyard of the old house in old Ténès. My mother, the Frenchwoman, seated on a chair near my father, lends out her children to be loved by these sisters, both of whom have no children. My mother smiles, watches the maternal scene multiplied by two, the embraces that wrap us up as though they were going to consume us, the laughter of a summer afternoon in the closed courtyard, protected by the aroma of the fig tree mixed with the honey cakes that we will take along for the trip back in the black Peugeot 202.

◇◇

And the women, the mothers of these wild boys who come to my father's school and who keep an eye out for us, my sisters and me, so that they can insult the Frenchwoman's daughters, the princesses under the high protection of their father, the principal, the native teacher. I see these women when they come on behalf of their sons to talk with my father in his language. I catch a glimpse of them when my sisters and I walk all the way to the colonial houses on the other side of the dry dirt esplanade. Behind the laundry that separates them from the gate and the street, they work, sitting in a circle on the ground. They chat, and if a child pulls the laundry too wide apart, they yell.

◇◇

Aïcha and Fatima live in the same courtyard behind the drying laundry. They share a windowless room that opens onto a dilapidated patio, and like the other women, they will have children, lots of children.

◇◇

The mothers in my books. Fictitious, imaginary mothers? I made the choice of a free, rebellious woman, while at the same time I discovered real women who were defiant, revolutionaries, and adventurers, in a time of chaos—Isabelle Eberhardt, Aurélie Tidjani, Alexandra David Neel, George Sand, Jane Bowles, Odette du Puigaudeau, Lou Andreas-Salomé, Annemarie Schwarzenbach, and Germaine Tillion, Germaine Laouste . . . It was at that precise moment that Berber, Arab, Muslim, illiterate, and sequestered mothers become the heroines of my books. The first mothers. Archaic, maternal mothers with large bodies wrapped in linens, where a child's body could get lost, mothers who speak the unknown language that doesn't give orders or worry about school or free will. I invent for myself a loving and warm mother who is always tender; this mother doesn't exist, I know that . . . I create a mother who is gentle with her daughters, a mother whom the teacher cannot change into someone who just gives lessons, or someone who forgets love because of duty.

"You'd like to have had an Arab mother . . ." Agnès Varda's words. I still hear them when the mothers of my father's people fill my books, as mothers.

The Silence of My Father's Language, Arabic

French colonial Algeria. I live on the school grounds, in the house my mother keeps at my father's school, the SCHOOL FOR INDIGENOUS BOYS, in Eugène-Étienne Hennaya, near Tlemcen. That's how I see it. Separated from the European neighborhood—the town center, where everything is laid out on a grid (schools, clinics, the town hall, the church, the kiosk, and the war memorial, which surround the town square, reserved for the French many times throughout the year, where there's the music of fanfares and dances on holidays)—at the end of a road that will never be paved, out toward the wine cellar and the colonists' farms, is the Arab neighborhood. We didn't say *"village nègre"* when we talked about the working-class neighborhood where the Arabs lived and where the Black African artisans lived before them, the masters of the tainted trades—butchers, blacksmiths, tanners . . . The skilled Black Africans, indispensable, scorned, mixed with the Berbers and Arabs, but colonial history, and then later nationalist and national history, forgot about them, just as France, the "Motherland," long forgot her infantrymen—Algerians, Senegalese, Vietnamese . . .

◇◇

Today by the shore in Fréjus, in the Var, we can visit a 1994 monument "dedicated to all the black troops who valiantly served under the French flag for more than a century and for whom Fréjus was the most important military camp." At the feet of the black soldiers lies a tribute from the African poet Léopold Sédar Senghor:

THE SILENCE OF MY FATHER'S LANGUAGE, ARABIC

TO THE BLACK ARMY
Passing,
they fell
fraternally united
so that you might remain French.

Since 1993 we've been able to walk the funereal path of the immense Memorial to the Wars in Indochina, where engraved lists align Arab, Berber, African, Indochinese, and some French names. We read them, we decode the exotic names, but we don't hear the languages. The soldiers are dead. On a stone slab, between the silent rows:

HERE LIE THE REMAINS OF
3152 SOLDIERS WHO DIED FOR
FRANCE IN INDOCHINA
1939–1954

These cemeteries are the colonial army's *"villages nègres,"* yet they are eternal, beautiful white marble villages.

◇◇

My mother's house isn't hers. It belongs to the French government, to Public Education, it's on the grounds of my father's school; my father: "the teacher from the countryside," "the little Arab man who was better than the little Frenchmen." He's a serious and inquisitive student of France's beautiful language, he's gifted in mathematics, he reads everything, he learns everything, he likes to recite poems that he discovers while learning the fluvial routes of France, this country of rivers where he'll meet a young Frenchwoman who is stunned to hear a young foreigner speak her language so perfectly and without the accent of Aquitaine. He doesn't look like the men from her native Dordogne; she listens to him, he speaks so well. On the parapet that runs along the Garonne in the city, they lean over the water, she sees his brown hand, brown like the ripened rye in her father's fields. I don't know what she thinks of this man's country and people. His eyes are blue. He wears round tortoise-shell glasses. He'll be a teacher. He won't take his young wife into the fortified citadel on the high Algerian plateaus, as Sid-Ahmed Tidjani, the great religious teacher of the Aïn-Madhi brotherhood, did. In 1870 this man met his wife, Aurélie Picard, from Champagne, in a hotel in Bordeaux, where the French government had taken refuge while fleeing German advances. My parents' citadel won't be Islamic; it will be secular. In 1940 their citadel was my father's school in Aflou, a village on the high plateaus of djebel Amour.

∞

From that year and until 1962, the year of Algerian independence, and even a few years after that, from city to city, all the way to Algiers, to Clos-Salembier, at each school my mother makes a home that become a little France built in the name of the French Republic. Surrounded by fences and walls, separated from the poor Arab houses, where the boys looking for spiritual and earthly food come from. Under the covered part of the courtyard my father feeds the boys. He's the first teacher to feed the "sons of the poor"; this would be their only meal all day. The other houses in the village are far from the school. On one side is the stadium, on the other is the dirt esplanade where the red peppers dry. There's a road that goes toward the orange groves and another that runs next to the wine cellar; this one might have gone all the way to the old, abandoned train station. My father takes this little France of secular teachers—himself and my mother—in hand. Within its walls, he guides it to become an ideal Republic where, in the name of justice, equality, and fraternity, the laws of learning are practiced in France's books, language, geography, and history. My mother raises us as little girls of the French Republic, and through France's language and books she transmitted a universal knowledge and a single language. Perfect little girls: we read the Countess de Ségur with enthusiasm—we're not Sophie; we're Camille and Marguerite instead—and the inspiring series about the Swiss girl Heidi. The France of books lives in our room. At home, no one speaks Arabic, the foreign language. We have the gestures and voice of my mother, the Frenchwoman from France. We don't have the local *pied-noir* accent that is crossed with corrupted French and Spanish. We speak the language of the books she gets from France. They are squeezed into two rows behind the library windows. We wear dresses that are tailored and embroidered like the ones in the fashion magazines to which my mother subscribes; she chooses plaid ribbons for our hair, a different color for each of the three sisters. We're the accomplished daughters of our teacher mother; this I say and repeat tirelessly, I write it . . . There's a piano in the house. My mother teaches us hygiene, French cooking, and etiquette. My mother's the best thing to come from the France of the Enlightenment and the Age of Reason.

◇◇

And my father? I think he's proud of his little France, which he takes with him from one job to the next, into the housing provided at different schools, housing that his wife ingeniously transforms into a warm and generous home. They congratulate him on the garden, the children . . . in French, never in the language of the "native" land. In his wife's home, my father doesn't speak his mother's language. He's an Arab, and yet I don't realize this. First and foremost, he's my father, attentive, present, patient (this is what his name means, but I haven't yet learned this), and a school principal. He magically resolves problems whose terms I read and reread without understanding the mathematical language, so foreign to me, so familiar to my father. I'm not surprised that he doesn't speak the Arabic of the street. Why would he speak it in the house of France that is now his home, where, without permission from his familial Muslim community, he founded a separate family, his family, with the foreign woman, in the foreign language, the language that, among other things, he passes on to the village children, the official language of law and order? A ruse by the Infidel of Nazarene to introduce doubt? Enclosed within the French school, these children will be strangers in their mother's land . . . Who considers this at that moment in time? Maybe my father's students, raised in the ways of France and sometimes in the ways of the French Revolution, already do, secretly organizing as nationalists for the next insurrection. Maybe some will walk from west to east after the Sétif massacres in May 1945, and nine years later the first French teachers from France will be their targets.

◇◇

My father doesn't speak to us in his language. He doesn't tell us about his people's legends, or about Djha, the sly little man who mocks the powerful and the despotic. Not a single book, not a single word in his language is to be found in the library. (I don't know if he knows the Koran by heart, or if he, like the other boys seated around the teacher, received lashings with the switch of olive wood, or if he wrote from right to left on the walnut board that his father passed on to him. This precious board was passed from father to son, but my father's oldest son won't inherit it; his illiterate sister keeps it next to the small *marabout* in the blue bedroom in old Ténès, the city where my father was born.) If a book had been lost behind the French books, I would've seen the shapes of the unknown language. Without knowing it, I would've recognized it. I searched so often for any books that would have been skillfully hidden, a sort of little "hell" I made. I found nothing, just illegible anatomy plates that I either didn't look at or just barely glimpsed.

◇◇

Aïcha, and later Fatima, the sisters from the poor houses who help my mother—they speak a domestic language reduced to words culled from housework, laundry, and ironing. My father translates my mother's directions and advice when the work goes beyond the ordinary tasks. From afar I can hear him talking at the back of the garden, near the laundry room. He speaks the maids' language. Is this his language? And from the mouths of boys, maybe Aïcha and Fatima's little brothers, young cousins who don't throw rocks at us, but rather words from a barbaric language. Is this my father's language? Insults, no doubt, and words I know get tangled up with them. Roumia and Roumiettes, the Frenchwoman, the Christian woman, the foreign woman, my mother, and we three, the daughters of this unwelcome woman, we who walk on the other side of the road that goes up toward the girls' school and French streets. Repeated a hundred times, the word, an aggressive, sexual one (I know this without knowing the word; it's the boys' devilish and lewd smiles that tell me that this word is taboo, and yet it's alright to use it against us, the daughters of the Frenchwoman), a weapon that strikes and kills, a knife that slits the throat and makes blood run, this brutal persecutory word, the pride of the boys. They are poor, but with their tremendous virile strength they could kill us. Before such a death and shame, the word hits, hurled by the boys, happy to humiliate and terrorize the three sisters walking silently, hand in hand, on hell's path. The word rolls, scolds, and bores in, leaping from one boy to the next until it reaches us: *fuck, fuck* . . . (I found this word again on the other side of the sea, unfurled in the projects where the sons and grandsons of those who yelled it at us now live. They left the fertile village that had become infertile, they lived in the *"cités nègres,"* the ghettos on the outskirts of town, and after moving into the shantytowns, their children colonized the French language. Is there a French person, young or old, who hasn't heard this word, whose sexual violence diminished as it crossed from Algeria to France, from the low-income housing projects to the city?). I know that I have already spoken and written about my silent astonishment at not daring to think that the language that sought to kill my sisters and me (several variations followed the street boys' Arabic words) was my father's language.

◇◇

No. My father speaks neither the maids' language nor the language of the wild boys who wounded us every school day. When I come home through the gate that separates us from the path of insults, I don't tell my father about these daily insults. A long time later, a very long time later, when my father was in exile in my mother's country and in the language he loves, he read what I wrote about how his language insulted us. He says nothing, just as he said nothing about his mother's house, his people, his language, his country, its history, its histories. Nothing. Obstinate silence on my father's side, the side of Arabic, of ancestral Algeria. The street boys tell me that my mother should be neither the teacher's wife nor my mother, that my father's house isn't her house, that Algeria is neither her country nor mine. By yelling this single word and delighting in this harassment, they mean that I'm not my father's daughter, that I'm not a part of his language or of his land, that my mother doesn't belong with Algeria's people. The boys destroyed the silence of the Arabic language. Intentional cruelty. If not, why such persistence every morning, year after year?

◇◇

On the first day of the insurrection in November 1954, they killed teachers, just like fifty years later, when brother killed brother. Were these the children of my father's language? The children educated in the school for indigenous boys, in the foreign, enemy language? Will they kill their teacher and massacre his godless, colonialist family? And what does my father say? Nothing. Not in French nor in Arabic. In the bedroom at home, my father and mother talk; they speak in hushed tones, but I can hear them. We don't ask questions; it's never the right time to ask questions. As for me, in the fortress of books and knowledge, shielded from the words that the sons of my father's people use, I silence what the Colony's young girls tell me in their denatured version of my mother's language. At times, varying the theme, they repeat the insidious questions whose perfidy I can't quite grasp (in an earlier essay I wrote about the everyday words of French Algeria's inquisition). My full name shows that I'm my father's daughter: my father, an Arab, an enemy of France, the scourge of the good and true French people, those industrious property owners of this uncultivated land rescued from ignorance, this land necessarily torn from its uncultivated language, its obscurantist religion, its obsolete customs. The young girls demand that I offer clear proof that I'm not my father's daughter. I stay silent. I don't know any artful ruses. My mother's language abandons me in a guilty silence, and my father's language, banished from the interior walls of the barbed-wired France, can't help me at all. Nor can my father and mother. Did my two sisters have to brave the same interrogations and hateful words in each language? (Even to this day I don't know. We could talk about it, but we don't.) I willingly removed myself from this life and moved into the life of books and novels translated from languages that are foreign to the Colony and to the war. I keep myself far away, ever farther away; in Russia before the October Revolution and then in American and Latin America, I use the language of my mother, the Frenchwoman, to shield myself from the language of my father, the Algerian.

◇◇

Books will never leave me. Coming back to my mother's language, the books I read didn't satisfy me. I avidly read French writers (why Proust at the same time as Céline?). I read in translation what my father's brothers write in Arabic, and beneath the French, I can hear the language of my father's mother; it isn't mute. I can hear it now, in secret, when I'm near the Arab women in the French low-income housing projects. I don't understand the meaning of the words, I only remember the voices of women speaking this language, women hidden from view in Hennaya, Algiers (Clos-Salembier and the Cité Nador), Blida (the Muslim quarter), Aïcha and Fatima's sisters and cousins, the women of my father's people. I didn't know what they said inside their courtyards, hidden by the laundry drying on the line, behind the open gate. I want to listen to my father's mother and sisters, who could barely be seen in the small courtyard with the fig tree and jasmine in old Ténès. (I spoke about them in an earlier essay, they will return to me.) I want to hear them and write about them in my mother's language, in order to reach my father and the silence of his language, Arabic, my father's Arabic.

∞

I write. Books. I write about the violence of imposed silence, exile, and separation, I write about my father's land, colonized, mistreated (even today), and savagely deported, I write in my mother's language. This is how I'm able to live, in fiction, the daughter of both my father and my mother. I trace my Algerian routes in France.

The Return of the Absent One

It was both dark and lifeless. Unable to see anything, unable to stay put while waiting for the break of day, and, just before dawn, perhaps a sliver of moon keeps you from getting lost . . . Yet it's the impenetrable night and emptiness where nothing and nobody can live. An immense black land, inhospitable, flat, and without beauty. A barrenness that terrifies.

That was me. A desolate landscape where nothing could happen, where nothing will happen because this landscape offers no unevenness to attract notice or halt a step, not a single peculiarity that draws interest. Not even fallow land. Fallow land promises surprises, though they are left untended. Darkness without hell. A desert without prophecy. Because I don't know anything about God, nor about his followers, nor about the sacred word delivered by a divine voice, the sacred word that the swords and stories of the victorious and the suffering spread throughout the desert beyond the seas. No one told me the stories of Abraham, Agar, Moses, Mary, Jesus, Mohammed. I will at last understand the story of Abraham and his sons Isaac and Ishmael when I weigh the meaning of sacrifice (he would have slit their throats had it not been for the magical intervention of the sheep), that total or partial immolation of man's body for his God.

∞

I don't know that prayer exists and that I can commune with God through the intimacy of a singular and coded word. I don't know that confession exists and that I can, in principle, speak with an attentive and benevolent intercessor. I don't know that self-reflection exists in the form of introspection and that this practice demands rigor and perseverance. I don't know how it is that I exist. I'm a person, of course. But the "I" is prohibited. No one says this, but I know it. In spite of myself, I follow the implicit command to deny the self, but this has nothing to do with self-denial, taking up God's word, his commandments, and his perfection. Put simply, memory is blank and empty, without a religious or familial inscription to give it depth, a real, tangible thickness, a stratified ground that can be decoded by reading the geological and genealogical strata. Nothing is said, but the "I" is banned, from both sides, maternal and paternal. I hear about republican Universalism and the Honor of the tribe, in spite of the silence, the silences. The intimate, the self with the self, in secret, without sonorous voices, with neither god nor master, in full solitude. With the other, not a word about the self. And with which other man or woman? Not with the brother, he's too far away, locked in the world of men, the first son, the only son, the oldest; nor with the sisters, mute like me, even today; nor with friends; there are no friends in which to confide. There is no patio at home, no closed courtyard, protected from the foreign street and from onlookers who don't have the right to see women spending time together. There are no women free from surveillance, chatting as if they're in the *hammam*'s hot rooms, where they laugh over bawdy stories and cry over the bloody misfortune of the wedding night.

◇◇

No joyous nor tragic patio, no indiscreet, humid *hammam*, only the small tiled courtyard where the principal's children play, sisters with sisters, without the boys' words. Smart little girls, obedient and polite. The teacher from France's daughters, my sisters and me, "the oldest of the girls"; we were so carefully raised, with neither exuberance nor sentimentality. On the other side of the house was the schoolyard. Forbidden to us every day save Sunday, it was immense and empty; we'd no longer hear boys shouting, just the whispers of sisters under the canvas tent, between the mulberry and hackberry trees. They don't tell secrets. The tent, in the austere courtyard, separates them from their brother, from the poor, rowdy boys and their sisters in long skirts with scarves tied at their forehead, little Arab girls who will never come to play in this camping tent that was put up for the principal's daughters, not for them. Together they'd have played hopscotch, pick-up-sticks, jacks, and foursquare on the red earth alongside the rooms of our home at the school.

◇◇

We must learn how to say and write "I." But what if no one is there to help it come to life so that this unknown "I," born of an unknown father and mother, can live and prosper? An orphan of the maternal "I" and of the paternal "I." How, from this double absence, can we produce the presence of an "I" that has been deprived so? There isn't a word in French for a mother or father who has lost a child. What do we call the woman who has lost her own "I," her "I" that certainly must exist? But not knowing whether or not it is gone, we must mourn and pass through the deepest grief. It would have disappeared; it would have been made to disappear because it was so frightful, so demonic . . . If it disappeared, like the young who are left to die on the battlefield, in the mud, we start to look for it in secret, regardless of the obstacles or whether it's forbidden. But how many detours before this audacity overcomes hesitation and profound reserve. Hesitation, reserve, restraint to the point of asphyxiation and amnesia. How—by what miracle—did the memory of these "I"'s, of this "I," return to me? By what game of mirrors did those things that I neither knew nor experienced

ARABIC AS A SECRET SONG

on the other side of myself, on the other side of my native body and my father's land, appear? Algeria, so far from France, separated by the sea, a very wide waterway that divides, but it's as though we can always see the other shore, whether the sky is light or dark. In order to navigate the numerous detours whose appearances sometimes deceive, there must be a break. Without violence. Consensual.

◇◇

The war continues. Active terrorism on the part of the secret army (the OAS, opposing Algerian independence) hits the Muslims first. I learned later that my father, head of the large school in Clos-Salembier, a working-class Arab neighborhood, appears on the blacklist, maybe along with his friend Mouloud Feraoun (who will be assassinated the night before his country's liberation). With my younger sister, I leave Algiers, my father and mother, my brother, and my other young sister. One sister will go into the sciences, the other into literature. It's as though I fainted; I live without myself. Algeria doesn't exist, nor do I. I'm not there. Shut inside of Algiers in the citadel of books, of school, I wrote frenetically in a little girl's journal, writing words from novels, sentences, whole pages from these stories that never took place near me, but rather on the other shore, next to the sea I don't see. I abandon the personal diary (it wasn't really that personal; I used other peoples' words, not mine). I'm not interested in myself. I don't see myself as a biographical subject. I don't think that my life is a book (I'd often heard others say this). What could I have written that would have been read? Nothing. What I don't know is that if I were to write those things that I'd never say (the secret part of me I'll never discuss), the story would be read. If I were to write, this isn't what I would write about. So I don't write. I read, far, very far. I've already said it, and I say it again: America, Russia, Nordic countries, all the way to the Mediterranean. No Algeria—I forget Algeria, I don't want to forget it; it's gone. It's been gone for a long time.

∝

I look elsewhere. Through space and time. Without knowing why exactly, I come to the triangular trade's Negroes and Negresses. Men, women, children captured, rounded up, sold. Deported from their African countries to North and South America and to the Caribbean islands. I follow their histories in long-forgotten novels in the National Library, on rue de Richelieu. Willingly sequestered in the dreary basements, I'm the feverishly happy reader. I follow them, from the bush to the slave ships' holds, from the slave auction to the wealthy white landowners' plantations. I hear them singing and crying in their language. I listen to them, to their work, to their pleas, to their revolt, and to the masters' cruelty and occasional kindness. Why did I choose them as protagonists in my somnambulist's life, the most foreign of foreigners, the black, illiterate slave man, the absolute Other, and the slave woman, who isn't any more familiar to me. If someone asks me why I read these books that might otherwise never have been read, I say that I don't know why. I think I'm telling the truth. I have the impression that the library, with its basements, cellars, and stacks and its passageways, resembles an immense drifting ship. I'm the one who wanders, not knowing where I'm going, where I am, on which continent, beyond the sea, beyond the Atlantic, from one sugarcane plantation to another, between indigo and coffee, aware of the field-workers' bodies—men and women—sweaty and toiling under the eye of the overseer with the whip. Why do I want to watch this spectacle of the slave trade and slave labor? Why do I read the Black Code and the registry of slave names? The distress of mothers separated from their children and of lovers who never married—they had to avoid creating a couple or making a family. Body, soul, and labor are the white man's property, that's the law . . . I stop in Saint Domingue (later, Haiti), a French Caribbean possession, the most prosperous island, pride of the colonial empire, until the slave revolt, the first one, both magnificent and barbaric, it's victorious (for who hasn't heard of Toussaint Louverture?). Saint Domingue is free, all of the Dominicans, white and black, are "free and equal under the law" (in spite of an attempt in 1802 to reestablish slavery, in spite of General Louverture's capture and death in a French prison in the Jura Mountains).

∞

I don't know yet that within Saint Domingue's history I'm reading about the oppression of Algerians and, later, about the Algerian insurrection that lasted until independence in 1962 (when I'm no longer in Algeria). I find out at the end of this work that is relentless, without any apparent reason for being so, that my father is Adonis, *le bon nègre,* the good colonial subject who didn't join the resistance (even though I know that the French army arrested and imprisoned him for his involvement in a network that distributed medical supplies—this was in 1957; I was living at home in my father's school in Blida), a good colonial subject who taught the French language to "indigenous boys" in the colonial Republic's schools. The Rights of Man and the benefits of social advancement. Some of his students would become *mujahideen,* freedom fighters, and the future cadres of the Algerian State, he knows this. I know, through these years of austere studies and immense solitude, that I'm my father's daughter; he was the good colonial subject. A man serving both his country and the French language. In exile both here and there. Now I know that exile is transmitted, that I'm in exile from myself. Perhaps divided from the start, daughter of the colonized, of my father; daughter of the colonizer, of my mother. I don't want to know whose daughter I am. I would be denying either my father or my mother if I had to choose. I don't choose. They tell me that I'm not my father's and my mother's daughter, they tell me that I'm my father's daughter or my mother's daughter. Why would I be born of the father or of the mother and not of both, a man and a woman, like every other child? I prefer to be an orphan.

◇◇

Then I get caught up in the turbulence of May '68 and the Women's Movement in Paris. I demonstrate with other men and women to defend universal values threatened in Vietnam by the American army (without also understanding that the Soviet Union, while helping the oppressed, represses its own citizens within the Soviet empire; the triumph of communism isn't a victory for freedom and equality—the coming years will cruelly reveal this). In the streets of Paris, I protest against the authoritarianism of power, society, the university, and, with women, against the social and political violence they endure, sexism and flagrant inequalities (even today it's necessary to defend the rights of women throughout the world). These struggles, these collective protests, draw me in. I believe that they are just, and I'm not alone, I'm all women, all the marginalized people, all the colonized people of the Empire and of the French interior. It's exhilarating. I'm no one in particular. I have no family, no father, no mother, no country. No one asks me who I am, whose daughter I am, where I come from, what my social position is. I'm a citizen of a spontaneous generation, I'm not alone. I have a political tribe, a utopia . . . Soon, I'll become, like the others, an orphan of the Revolution, but with women I reflect, I speak, I talk openly. Metaphor of the hidden patio. We start a journal, *Histoires d'Elles* (Women's histories)—three unique, exuberant years—and Xavière Gauthier's review, *Sorcières* (Sorceresses), gives freedom to words. It's then that the memory of Algeria comes back to me, through its Arab women rather than through my mother, the French teacher of my childhood.

◇◇

Algeria will never leave me. I'll be born to myself (I'll need many years, hundreds of pages) out of the union that stuns me without blinding me, Algeria with France, my Algerian father with my French mother. A history so unique, so strange, and so discreet that I'm just barely beginning to wish to be able to speak and write about it. But I haven't come to it without detours. Because the story of the family saga, along the shores of the Dronne River, where my mother was born, along the shores of the sea, where my father was born—this story has no memory. No narrative, no legend, no mythology that breathes life into the young minds of the children born of these silent crossings. The private history is obliterated at the same time as the public one. It's war, the war for Algerian liberation, that, for me, makes the story. With the war I take leave of the nothingness.

◇◇

Without knowing why, nor what I seek in the capital city and in the peripheral ones, I walk from one square to another, a patio displaced from the maternal shore to the shores of exile. I stop near the women sitting on the benches, near the dirty, gritty sands where small children play. They talk among themselves, voluble in my father's language and in the other one, the language of the Berber mountains. I can't always distinguish between the two; French words mix in with the foreign languages. Sometimes young girls, sisters, approach the mothers in the square. They talk to one another in the language of the French school, they laugh with the women. I hear them, I listen to them, I understand the gestures, the looks, the laughs, but not the languages, but it's as though none of their words escaped me, as though I'd always been talking with them. They become *Fatima ou les Algériennes au square* (Fatima or the Algerian women in the square), the first Fatima of France's French literature, the first literary Algerian woman, immigrant, illiterate, the first of the women of the tribe of my father, he who never belonged to a tribe. (Whenever he agreed to answer my questions, my father told me that his ancestors were descendants of the Prophet Mohammed. Which Arab isn't descended from the Prophet? They weren't the tribe's leaders. I thought I understood that my father considered the noble townsmen superior to any tribal leader, even to the most famous leader, but he didn't say so.)

∞

With Fatima, I start to fill my books with all of my father's Arab women. My father, Muslim and monogamous, who for more than half a century was in love with a Frenchwoman who was born in France. I never met these Arab women, I don't know them, I've never spoken with them. Veiled women, unveiled in exile—I see these women as though I were veiled, sheltered, a single eye visible under the white *haïk* made of wool and silk, the most beautiful one, the one belonging to my father's mother and sisters, in Ténès. I go, an invisible and weightless phantom, one eye free. An eye more curious than the gaze of the Colony's Nazarene photographers upon the women they referred to as "Fathma" in the captions of lucrative postcards, an eye so curious that it reads what isn't to be read, grasps what is hidden, and understands what others don't. It's as if I had been born in their home. I'm the daughter of my father's people, by way of their mothers—the body of the native land, my father's land, my land, and my body—in the language of my mother, the beloved foreigner.

∞

Fatima has daughters, both real and fictional. Shérazade and the others. Shérazade lives in a romantic trilogy: *Shérazade, 17 ans, brune, frisée, les yeux verts* (Sherazade: Missing, aged 17, dark curly hair, green eyes); *Les carnets de Shérazade* (Shérazade's notebooks); and *Le fou de Shérazade, entre Orient et Occident* (Mad about Shérazade, between Orient and Occident). I invent the heroine of a modern tale. Algeria's daughters in France, France's daughters connected to Algeria, these daughters crossing back and forth, like me. But the paper daughters are more intrepid: they run away and invent their young life in a utopian space, utopia's country is nowhere, the byways between the maternal house and France's house, sites of encounters that are both happy and unfortunate, sites of all crossroads, of all dangers. The daughters, with the brothers or against them. The sons and daughters who have left, traveling far geographically or going to prison, to drugs, to war. Momo, *le Chinois vert d'Afrique;* Jaffar in love with Lise, Shérazade's companion in the Orient; Julien, *le fou de Shérazade;* Melissa on the balcony with the lemon trees in Algiers; Amel and the Algerians who disappeared in the Seine on October 17, 1961, in Paris; Marguerite and Sélim; the French photographer who died because he loved Mériéma . . .

◇◇

To come back to myself, to say "I," I had to walk a long way, to talk and live at a distance at once real and close to the imaginary, I had to hear, far from the native land, everywhere where it was spoken, the voice of my father's language, the Arab voice, the foreign language, the intimate foreigner. In plazas, in parks and gardens, in town squares, under the plane trees, on benches, at the foot of war memorials. In the Arab cafés in Barbès, Montreuil, Belleville . . . in the metro cars, along the construction sites, behind the green garbage trucks with "Paris Sanitation" written on the side, by the trucks that spit out tar. In the cities in need of labor, those ogresses, Marseilles, Clermont-Ferrand, Lyon, Mulhouse, Strasbourg, Paris, Lille, Rouen, Nantes, Bordeaux, Toulouse, Perpignan, Ajaccio . . . , and in the French regions, Bouches-du-Rhône, the Rhône valley, Alsace, Lorraine, Nord-Pas-de-Calais, Seine-Maritime, Île-de-France . . . There, where the fathers and the grandfathers came, young and determined, working for France and the family back home, sending money orders, each month at first and then not at all. Now old men, these *chibanis* await death, abandoned, there where the mothers, who rejoined their spouses after having been alone for too long, brought into the world the sons and daughters of another land, and from that moment on, in another language, children separated from the maternal body, from the ancestral home; these children fill my stories, making up an immense new tribe. In this way I invent, year after year, a new family. I write of the displaced body of my father, his land, in my mother's language, and I hear the voices, the laughter and the shouts, the words that intersect. Violence, hatred, tenderness, love . . . I don't forget the image, everything that calls to me, the traces of memories that play on unusual, unexpected, and unclear connections: the inscriptions with arabesques, the colors of the Orient in the gaze of the Occident, the North African women on postcards (they will make the trip around the world, these photographs, in black and white, in sepia, in color), the shocking portraits of women in the war taken by the soldier photographer, the Algerian women of female French ethnographers, young, knowing adventurers traveling on the back of mules in the Aurès and the Kabylie mountains.

◇◇

So many detours, intended and unintended, to come back to myself with the complicity of the extended tribe in France . . . So I no longer back down, I no longer believe in an indecent secret that must be hidden, I know that I can, at last, say "I" with neither exhibitionism nor obscenity, without hurting my mother or betraying my father. No mercenary performance of selling myself. I return to my childhood in the Colony, to my family, father and mother, brother and sisters, to the native village and the land, to my people, to me, the distance in time and space abolished. I went so far away, and now I've come back.

To Hear Arabic as a Sacred Song

My father voluntarily placed me on my mother's side, the side of the conqueror, the side of power, of France in Algeria, of French Algeria through its language and its books, obstinately. Conforming to my father's wishes, I didn't learn his language, and I write and say that I'll never learn it. He granted my mother hospitality in his land, and she granted him hospitality in her language. But what was granted to me? I only got scenery, the scenery of childhood, and it's from this place that I write. But this scenery is impoverished, for no language, no voices live there. By passing through the language of the adored foreigner (my mother) and the adored language (French), my father could have, but never wanted—or maybe he thought it a kidnapping?—to wrest a child away from the mother's milk and swaddle this child in the foreign language, the Arabic of his own mother, his infancy, his childhood, his religion. And he didn't tell me the stories of Djha, the cunning little man of great wealth and power, nor the legends of his village, Ténès, nor the family epic, of which I know nothing except that the family is descended from the Prophet, which accounts for its nobility (but what proof is there? the line is broken, and the infidel in the house unseated the oldest son, losing his birthright for him), nor of the secret history (but why secret?) of his country, Algeria without France (like a forbidden, subterranean history that will rise up later with a force bordering on madness, a startling violence that I never cease exploring from detour to detour, from variation to variation).

◇◇

A silence, silences like so many sacred gifts of love to the foreign woman? Can a voluntary amnesia this absolute be generous? Or is this allegiance really a way of submitting to the conqueror? Was it the desire of this missionary couple, advancing secular education, not to disturb the little France constructed in an ideal, republican isolation? After founding this minuscule utopian city, my father kept the promise of generous love; he didn't desert France's home after having deserted his mother's language and home. I don't see my father as oppressed, as a victim of colonial France. Deprived and corrupted, no. My father took up the arms of the language of seduction, the language of the Revolution and his wife, the very young Frenchwoman who was fine and elegant, a foreigner who had dazzled him at a ball in that city where the Garonne River flows, in the land of rivers. My father betrayed neither the host language nor his mother's land. He defended the motherland from within the adopted language, his children's language, the language in which the values common to Islam and the Enlightenment revolutionaries were passed on. Because values cross into one language, they can be translated into another. Everything can be translated; teachers and People of the Book know this and make it known. My father knew this, and I know it. He could have taught me his language; anything can be learned, I also know this. My father withheld his language, along with its legends and songs (nursery rhymes are for nannies and older relatives caring for the very young), epics and Arab poetry. I wrote this once before, now I'm writing it once again; this is how my father resisted France, his foreign wife, his children, his descendants. His silence was his resistance. I'm no longer hypothesizing when I affirm this, when I write this down. Yes, by making it inaccessible, my father preserved his language, and with it, everything of the Algeria where I was born.

◇◇

TO HEAR ARABIC AS A SACRED SONG

The enigma of my birth, a foreign man with a foreign woman in the unique and beautiful language of the Frenchwoman, my mother, the enigma of the absent language that my father keeps secret just behind the language shared by the family he brought into the world—these enigmas are the subjects of my books. They are literally sacred gifts of silence. They make me the writer that I am, my father's scribe. I give him a gift, not knowing how he would receive it, nor if he would have wanted to receive it, if he would have received it (he read my books, though he never said anything to me about them, apart from saying I could sign them with his name). When he was still able to read, sick in Nice, he read and reread, without talking about it, one of my books, *Le silence des rives (Silence on the Shores)*, a sort of *tomb* for my father, this book where death is so present, along with the piercing questions regarding death in exile when people don't die surrounded by their mother's language. My father died far from the Arabic of the house in old Ténès, far from his mother's tomb in the little graveyard by the sea, without the sacred voice of the prayers for the dead, without the ritual gestures that accompany an Islamic funeral. He often said that a Muslim, no matter what happens, no matter what he does, whether there be a crisis or a lapse, remains a Muslim. My father didn't have a Muslim death; even though he rests under the shade of a fig tree, it's a foreign fig tree, and the cemetery isn't in Muslim lands. I give my father beyond the tomb something he perhaps might not have wanted, something that would have kept him in the tradition. His wife would have been a cousin, chosen for the eldest son by his mother—the best, the most beautiful, the most accomplished cousin. He would have been a good student at the *madrasa*. Carrying on the most beautiful and free-flowing Arabic, he would have honored the memory of his ancestors and the family's *marabout,* the family's saint. His mother and sisters wouldn't have lived in a state of noble poverty, the poverty of those families disinherited by colonization and predatory cousins. I give my father the imaginary tribe that I believe he might not have wanted, a tribe on paper, a fragile tribe without the immortality of flesh and bone.

∞

My father kept me far from these women, but their voices still reached me, and I went looking for them on the other shore. They were there, in body and word, and I discovered them, behind the curtains in secret houses and in foreign studios where curious and fascinated photographers came to steal their beautiful images. They are there before the eye that seeks them (my father wouldn't have looked at them the way I do). I heard them, in my father's language, patient and quiet, from across squares, in the towers and the low-rises of the low-income housing projects. They still wore flowered dresses and scarves—hills, mountains, and plateaus removed to the foreign shore, in the foreign language—and at their sides are children who will soon enough wish never to see their mothers' flowers in front of the school, the clinic, or the city hall, nor hear the words they believed to be the words of the impoverished (who will be there later on to tell them otherwise?). To the father who kept me from them, I give these women, his people's women, this people that he left (he defended their freedom during the war of independence, but he left them). These women with whom I haven't lived, they've lived in me as though I was born with them, as though I carried them within me. I believe that I do carry them and that they speak to me in a language that I hear without understanding. I have the sound, I don't need the meaning, it's already there. I know what they're saying, what they're saying to one another, I don't believe I'm mistaken. They whisper their words to me. An angel on my right, an angel on my left, they're my angels. Perhaps my father would've refused these women I'm giving him, refusing the role of patriarch and the constraints of ancestral obligations, therefore refusing to deprive his daughters of school, books, knowledge reserved for boys, or else he would have needed a sizeable fortune, which he didn't have, to afford private tutors at home.

◇◇

I don't offer my father his people on his land and in his language; rather I offer him fragments of the Algerian body wrapped in the silence of exile, in exile from the other language and from his hospitable school, on his wife's French side of the shore, his wife who returned to her native land without ever having left her own language. Perhaps the sea—it was the sea of his childhood in Ténès, the circular sea, indivisible—perhaps the sea rolled the maternal accent just as it did my father's contented body swimming in the Mediterranean? He refused to leave its shore. And when he shut himself away in the humble house in beautiful France, in my mother's Dordogne, with its own rivers, he would sit on a flat stone, his rock under the trellis, and read. What he read, I will never know, but the man of books that he was made me think of the young man meditating under the one-hundred-year-old olive tree on the hill facing Cap Ténès. My father gave his children to his wife, to France, to the language of love, which he welcomed like the model teacher. He gave her the best and his youth, his enthusiasm for an idealistic republic, his longing for justice and equality. Couldn't he be this just individual in my mother's language? Could it be that this language was there, present like a twin sister, and I didn't know? I still don't know?

◇◇

I translate Algeria, I translate my father into my mother's language. I invent him, I invent for myself an immense family on both sides of the sea. In this way I believe that I'm mending a broken chain. I'm giving my father this chain. I'll never know how he would have received it. Will the reader, in place of my father, find out? Will this reader tell me? I haven't yet met this person. That would end this unrest. Serenity? I'd no longer write.

I'll add, as it just occurred to me, that my father's language, absent, heard, lost, recovered, never spoken, his language is there in spite of this intentional silence. It's there, like sediment; no one can take it from me. I hear it like music, like a sacred language. I know death is there; it's mine. And the books that I've written aren't enough. Someday they'll all leave their shelves, public or private. Where will they end up? Recycled paper, book sales, with the used-book sellers at best, and be read again . . . They will also end in dust, it's possible, dust to dust. This Arabic language that myself and others, for a long time, saw as foreign, sometimes hostile and dangerous, my father's Arabic provokes emotion, a deep song in my mother's language. I waited for Arabic to come to me, and it came, supple and round, with its burst of laughter and fury. It came, and I welcomed it. As my father welcomed France's language, I welcome this foreign language from the native land. I want it to be foreign, with the familiar and complicitous distance of love, the Arabic of the beloved foreigner, my father.

I Write of Arabic, Foreign at Home, and of God, Foreign at Home

The daughter of teachers, a father and a mother, both secular supporters of the Republic from their first school through their last, from Aflou, the village on the high Algerian plateaus, where the Vichy regime relegated my father, to the city of Algiers and the large school in Clos-Salembier, a working-class neighborhood where the riots against the colonizer, and later against the single-party Algerian government, began . . .

◇◇

The daughter of these teachers, both missionaries of the French Republic and its literature, teaching the Colony's Muslim children how to read and write, and in our home were the books, dictionaries, and encyclopedias. For us children—my brother, the oldest, and my two younger sisters—there were books and more books. We learn to read with illustrated children's books, we read books from France. In the books were France and other foreign countries as far away as Sweden, America, Russia, but never Algeria. There was Science Literature Art, the legends of Athens and Rome, ancient Egypt, Ashur and Sumer, Timur and Marco Polo . . . No Arab or Berber tales, no *Tales of the Arabian Nights,* no life of the Prophet Mohammed, no saints of Christian history. I never saw the Virgin when I was young, I didn't see Christ hanging on the cross, I didn't see the Virgin Mother crying over her son Jesus' body, crucified to death.

In the family library and on nightstands, neither the Bible nor the Koran. God doesn't dwell in our home. I hear the church bells, Joy and Sadness, the sounds of the *muezzin*'s chant, his calls to prayer, but I don't ask questions. God isn't in my life, neither in places of worship, nor in religious rites; God doesn't concern me, I don't hear him, I don't speak to him. Who would have taught me how? God is absent from the books I read, and I read all the time. I don't choose my books, my father and mother choose them for us, nothing is missing from them—life love death—but God, no, he isn't in there, he never was: I don't miss what I don't know.

At our home on the school grounds, I know that anything can be learned, but no one teaches me about God. My father was raised Muslim, my mother was a little Christian girl. I don't know that my father is Muslim, I don't know that my mother is Christian. I don't see anything in the house that would suggest that they were. I don't hear words against religion, or religions. At what point had it ceased to exist, for how long? I still ask myself this question, having written the books that I've written.

◇◇

I learn the commandments of that secular, republican morality that came from the Enlightenment and the French Revolution of 1789; some of them are contained within the Ten Commandments, but I'm not aware of it. I'm a perfect little girl, my sisters too. We are obedient, helpful, reserved, modest, studious. I don't steal, I don't hit my neighbor, I'm good, but I don't fear God, I don't pray to God. What exactly is prayer? I still don't know. I'm not covetous, I'm not greedy, I'm not a liar, I don't incite anger, I pity poor children—there are a lot in colonial Algeria, I see them every day—I know that I will eat and that it will be good (my mother is a fine Périgordian cook), that I will be clean and that I will have pretty clothes (a seamstress comes to my mother's house every Thursday), that I will sleep between sheets that smell good, I know that I have a father and mother who love me . . . At confession I wouldn't have anything to confess. Much later I will learn that confession exists, I will hear my friends and my fellow activists who are working to raise social consciousness in the Women's Movement speak about the constraints imposed by nuns in parochial schools. I will hear of their suffering and their revolt. Much later still I will hear Algerian women in the squares, in exile, in France, punctuate the crises and rumors of the housing projects with prayers to Islam's God.

∞

When we take long trips in my father's black Peugeot 202, from our house to the sea, I see the Algerian countryside, the fields that have been cultivated and harvested, the farms, the vineyards and the orange groves, the cooperative wine cellars smelling of grape must, the worn hills, the hedgerows of cactus surrounding the poorhouses, the young shepherds with a few animals, some sheep and goats, the wild children screaming at the passing car, and often women wrapped in white, their veils pressed against their faces, walking together toward the saint's *marabout,* the saint's tomb. That's how my grandmother and her daughters would visit the family shrine on the butte not far from Ténès, my father's birthplace. Illiterate with respect to God, religion, rites, and dogmas, I knew nothing of the fervor of these women in white, nor of the fervor of my father's mother and sisters. I watched the women's procession to the isolated little *koubba,* the green or bluish dome; sometimes there's an olive tree leaning against a wall, or an old vagabond woman sitting on the threshold. I saw all of this at the speed of the Peugeot 202. Between the villages I would watch these unknown women surrounding a Muslim tomb, kneeling in prayer, their veils filled with the evening wind. They spoke or recited prayers; there were red geraniums piously placed at the head and the foot of the stone tomb.

∞

Why, not knowing their God, did words addressed to God, spoken by rural Algerian woman who shared the same faith, women walking together toward the holy mausoleum, why did they provoke such emotion within me? I can't hear them, they're far from me, but I hear them. I don't ask my father questions. It seems that I don't want anyone to come between these women and me. I don't see the faces they uncover when it's hot; they pass a thin white handkerchief over their forehead and neck, but it's as though I saw them. I recognize them today, in the books I write; I call those women my foreign sisters, the women of my father's people.

These women living in poorhouses on the side of the hill, bowing in communal prayer in the cool room, golden because of the sun's last light, the misery of daily life doesn't touch them. That's what I believe when I'm caught by this élan toward these women whom I will never approach when they're on their happy pilgrimage—but perhaps some day, because fiction and the imaginary have this divine quality for a writer: they work miracles in what we call books. These women of my father's people, poor, illiterate, and Muslim, they fill my books with their simple faith and their beliefs. I haven't lived with them. I haven't shared bread and salt and water with them. I haven't spoken with the Muslim women on the hill, by the holy *marabout*. I saw them so little, my father's mother and sisters, in the small courtyard with the fig tree, maybe three times during my childhood; after that there was the war. After the war, the departure. They would never be there again, nor the women with their *haïk,* the white veil, the graceful gestures that held the shifting veil, their steps, the folds of fabric moving with the evening breeze. When they return to the village, I hear them laughing and talking, their voices are high-pitched and loud, no one watches them or listens to the words drifting over the plains. I didn't know it then, but I love these women, I search so wildly for them, without having the words to converse with them on the other side of the shore.

∞

Being the teachers' daughter that I am, the girl without God who watched the Sisters, the nuns, go by, with white and blue headpieces tight around their foreheads, long pleated canvas skirts covering their ankles, and sturdy leather sandals that the village shoemaker made especially for them and for their long walks in the countryside. Near the church, they ran the clinic and the workshop where the little Muslim girls, who were rich or orphaned, who didn't go to school, learned how to sew, embroider, and weave. The orphans worked on the trousseaux of the rich girls whose fathers mistrusted the colonizer's secular education. They bought fashionable fabrics in the city; it was expensive. The girls also embroidered the trousseaux for the young girls of the colonists' large agricultural domains. The Colony's young girls would have grandiose weddings; these poor little girls would help in the kitchens on such days. Nobody would know how hard they had worked to intricately embroider the sheets and shirts for these young women, they would see the beautiful linens hung out behind the masters' homes, they would recognize the embroidered sheets, shirts, napkins, and tablecloths that their mothers had scrubbed on the washboard in the large steaming wash boiler.

∞

I knew nothing of these women, of their choice of religion, of their Christian mission. They resembled neither the Muslim women nor the women from the colonial village who danced on the kiosk's stage for the July 14th celebration. My mother also danced with my father; people must have watched the Frenchwoman and the Arab man with the talkative curiosity of the

South. The Sisters—we called them sisters—would stride along the dirt road to the agricultural domains of the fertile plain. Maybe one of them helped deliver the babies of the farmworkers' wives in the houses of the nearby *douar,* just as the White Sisters did, those missionaries of the high Algerian plateaus where I was born. They must have taught catechism to the Christian children. As for us, there in the courtyard of the girls' school in the European village's square, we didn't talk about the life of Jesus. I never went into the village church. I found the little girls in my class who took their First Communion to be pretty, but I didn't envy them. I didn't eat at their table after the ceremony; they didn't invite me.

◇◇

And then came exile, far from the tombs of Muslim saints and the village church, after a revolution in which God hardly had any place at all. To fight for the liberation of a country or to hold on to lands that had been worked by the very ancestors buried under the tall, black cypress trees, lands yet to be worked by fathers who were still alive, this is not a battle for God.

In exile, where Algeria doesn't exist, I shut myself away among shelves of books that no one has read for a long time, whole days spent at the National Library on the rue de Richelieu, getting the titles from the library catalogue, then going through the collection of eighteenth-century French colonial books and stories. I go backward from the conclusion of a long period of colonization—Algeria is now independent—to the beginning of a more barbaric era, one started in the name of the Cross and economic gain, in the Caribbean islands: They deport African slaves to plantations, Christianize black men and women but don't educate them; these people might revolt . . . they will revolt.

◇◇

At the same time, I read the Lives of Saints without a detour through the commentaries, I don't want auxiliaries, I read by decoding, like an illiterate person, I struggle, but I persevere. I start with the New Testament. I believe that I'm reading the life of Jesus, but I don't actually read the life of Jesus. I read an easy text without understanding anything; it's as if I'm reading a foreign language. The perfect little girl doesn't give up. I read the Old Testament. It's less severe, more violent, with its family stories, tribal stories, tales and legends, epics, poems of love and death . . . I still don't know who God is, and when I read the Koran, I don't know him any better than I did before. I read, but I tire, so I accept the ancillary books. I want to understand, so I read around God and religion and sacred texts. What I have retained, I couldn't say. Much later, I thought about these reclusive women, writers or poets, who were raised far across the Channel, on the Bible's milk, honey, and venom, and whose books I loved. The only book they had in the house, in any of the rooms, was the Bible. They would read it and reread it under their breath, out loud, without tiring; they knew how to read it—for them it was a divine literary miracle, they wrote.

◇◇

I didn't learn my father's language, Arabic; I didn't learn about God. My father didn't teach me his language; neither my father nor my mother taught me about God. They gave me books; I read all the books. But I don't know how to read my father's language, which was foreign at home, nor God's language, also foreign at home. I'll never know how, I know this; there's no remedy. It's with these missing pieces that I write.

◇◇

For a long time I wrote in ignorance of this particular lack. Today I write knowing it, but I also know that it's irreparable. No matter what I do, no matter what I read, no matter what I write.

Dedication, energy, perseverance, the virtues of the teachers' daughter, they all come to naught.

◇◇

And so I hear voices. The voice of my father's language. The voice of Muslim women, the voice of their Muslim gestures and their history with God, Allah, their fathers and mothers' God since the time of the Prophet of Islam, the voice of beliefs and of simple, everyday piety. These voices, I hear them, from the high plateaus, from the mountains and deserts, from the sides of ravines and hills with the saints' white-and-green *koubba,* all the way to the shantytown homes in the other country where the men, fathers, husbands, brothers, and cousins work, all the way to the low-income housing and modern homes. But where are the eucalyptus and olive trees, the fig trees on the slope by the stream, the geraniums for the graves and the basil? What happened to the pilgrimage to the saint's *marabout* and the light white veil, warm in winter, cool in summer? They see it all, they're invisible; the veil keeps the secret, all the secrets. In this country there's no veil, no *haïk;* only the old women, the very oldest women, wear it on the other shore. These voices, I translate them in my books.

◇◇

And what if my father's language, my father's Arabic, had disappeared with my father? If memory weakens, I'll no longer hear the voice of this foreign, beloved, unique language. But I hear it, I want to hear it, I go where I can hear it, I know where to go in this country where I now live my life. This country isn't my father's country, nor is it a country of Islam, but my father's Arabic lives on this side of the sea and it will live in my books, underground, patient, secret, I'd like to say sacred.

◇◇

And the women's voices? I no longer hear them. On both shores, the women of my father's people betrayed me. They betrayed my father, his language, and his Muslim faith. The white *haïk,* the traditional veil in Maghrebian Islam, the veil that marked opposition to colonization until victory, this veil has disappeared. With it, the voice and the gestures, the grace of the women I loved, who guided me toward the squares in the housing projects, the talkative, cheerful, quick-tempered Algerian women's conversations held on patios. The white veil is folded up at the bottom of suitcases, trunks, and closets; it will be the death shroud covering the Muslim corpse. The *hijeb* replaces the Islamic scarf, but it isn't alone. The full-length black *abaya* joins it, and sometimes black gloves. No more face, no more body, mechanical gestures of willing submission to edicts put forth by the new leaders of fundamentalist and political Islamic laws.

◇◇

I no longer know how to capture the voice of my father's Arabic, nor the Muslim voice of women, veiled in white, those who walked together on the dry hill toward the bluish mausoleum, the blue of the sky veiling its dome. It was a warm night when they went back down to the houses, running because of the slope and laughing like young girls.

I still write books. Perhaps they are silent.

I Write the Imaginary Arab, My Father

I often wonder why, while my father was alive, I didn't write *Je ne parle pas la langue de mon père* (I do not speak my father's language) or *L'arabe comme un chant secret* (Arabic as a secret song).

I must make clear that some texts included in *L'arabe comme un chant secret* were published in journals and my father could have read them. But someone would have had to inform him of their publication. I never sent him anything that appeared in a journal. He never read them, nor did my mother, except for one of them that accidentally arrived at their home; I found out because my mother didn't agree with what I had said about her at the time. I wouldn't write about her in the same way today; it was brutal and unfair. I hadn't understood my mother's tears or what could have hurt her (my mother is not someone who weeps: she is a woman and a Mother Courage embodied). Re-reading this text in 2010, I understand what escaped me back then. Without making any changes, I am republishing it some decades later because I know that my mother will not read it. It opens the second edition of this book.

◇◇

Do the daughters and sons who write reveal a secret or unknown family secrets? How should we write about our fathers or mothers, about a story concerning them, without having their permission? If they are alive, how much liberty should we take?

◇◇

I WRITE THE IMAGINARY ARAB, MY FATHER

I wrote, published, and signed my work with my father's last name, my birth name, what we call a "maiden name," without ever thinking, as did some of my friends (women writers with Algerian fathers), that I should use a pen name because I had become a public figure, making public my father's Arabic name in the other language, the French language of the colonizer. I didn't think that I should become another in order to preserve the honor of the tribe.

If my father ever belonged to a tribe, it was a long time ago; he had broken free of it, and I didn't know then that my father's family had descended from the Prophet. Anyway, would I have believed it? Maybe it's because I wouldn't have believed it that my father spoke so little about this noble lineage. He only mentioned it inadvertently, as though his children, born of the foreign woman and into the foreign language in his Arab and Muslim ancestors' land, but far from the prophetic ancestors' spirit, could only understand the family story as a legend. He knew, however, that children believe in legends and that they don't forget them.

∞

I sign my books with my father's name, Sebbar. I'm my father's daughter. I don't want to be a different daughter who writes and who signs with another name. When I asked him one day— I believe that I have already told this story, in one form or another, for this is how I write, with variations upon digressions, repeating, tireless—when I asked my father, after I had already published many books, as though I were sure of his answer, if I could sign with his name, he looked at me, ironically:

"You did it, and you never asked me."

"That's true. Many times."

"So, what's the point?"

"I don't know. I want to know what you think."

"What I think?"

"Yes. It's your name."

His blue eyes crinkled, as though they were smiling.

"You're my daughter. It's your name."

"Yes, but . . ."

"It's your name. You write what you want, my daughter. I trust you."

◇◇

How would my father have read the two books in which I continuously say that I write my father's body in my mother's language? He might have thought it was presumptuous to write, to speak through writing, about what we don't know. What's the risk? Betrayal.

◇◇

We say "to betray a secret." I think that I betrayed a secret precisely in these books. And is it because of this that my father shouldn't read them? A secret. What secret? What names are revealed that should've stayed within the family? Were there names that should be silenced because to expose them would be to expose the disgrace of collaboration with the enemy, of a murder carefully concealed, of a cowardly escape, of a bastard child . . . ?

◇◇

I wrote my father's name, my mother's maiden name, Bordas, a name common to the Dronne, the beautiful river in Dordogne. I wrote women's first names, the women of my father's people, Aïcha, Fatima. Did I write his sisters' first names? I don't think so. Maybe the name of the younger cousin, sometimes mute, sometimes talkative. My father would speak with her and they would laugh. Affectionate and happy, she touched us, the Frenchwoman's children. Surprised and amused by our dresses that were too short, by the ribbons that looked like butterflies in our hair, she looked at the embroidery on the collars of our dresses with the eye of an expert. Did she do the same thing with my father's sisters? I don't know if she was one of their daughters, or if she had been adopted. Did she finely embroider a trousseau for herself? Did she marry? Was she married off? Her children would've been cherished. I'll ask whoever might be able to answer me. And if I go to Ténès . . .

◇◇

To talk in this way about the women in my father's family, a family that an attentive reader from Ténès would be able to identify, is to go against the laws of Muslim decency; it's to act as a barbarian, ignorant of the rites and codes of a secular civilization. It attacks the dignity of a family and its women.

◇◇

I am this barbarian. I am illiterate.
    And I don't know it.

◇◇

If my father had left me his language, Arabic, as an inheritance, I would have written in Arabic, but I never would have written about my father in his own language. I proclaim this, and with great certainty. What I write of my father in French—the language that is foreign to his sisters and mother and that bars them from reading this story where they are living in the courtyard with the fig tree and jasmine in old Ténès—I wouldn't have written in Arabic, because my father wouldn't, in this case, have been this unknown figure in my books: the imaginary Arab man. The silence of his language, his silence in his language, brought forth, after a long amnesia, the profusion of words in the other language, obsessive to the point of insanity, a patient desire to know, the curiosity of a child from whom a secret is stubbornly kept and who looks for the key to the *cabinet noir,* so full of its own surprises, be it emptiness or blood.

◇◇

I go where I shouldn't, I say what shouldn't be said, I name what shouldn't be named. I say that my father gave his children to France, to his wife, to her language. Did he make this offering out of love? My father welcomed this interloper, the seductress; he gave himself to her, body and soul. He became another, but not an apostate. He often said in his final years that he was Muslim from his birth until his death. If God had so desired, he would have made the pilgrimage to Mecca alone, without his wife, without his children. I'd say instead that my father was a defector to the other side.

If a defector betrays, then my father betrayed. Am I the daughter of a traitor? This would be the great secret.

My father didn't give his mother's language to his children. He willingly kept it from me. Colonial history isn't the only reason for this act of holding back. I say it again, I write that he resisted in this way, setting us apart, out of danger. What danger? He kept the Arabic language far from me, not just from the home, but far to protect it, to protect himself. From us, his children? From his wife, my French mother? Was it so as not to be a traitor?

◇◇

It was so as not to betray *his people.* My father never said that. I didn't hear him say it in French. Maybe when he spoke with his Algerian friends, fellow supporters of Algerian independence, did my father say, just like they did, *my people, our people?* It was a question of a people, his people in his language, the language of his country, his land, his mother, a people to be liberated at the expense of the other language, the colonizing enemy language. This language also knew how to work for the people, for the French Revolution.

My father could say *my people,* which we were not, neither his children nor his wife. He could say it only at the moment when he was another, like so many men and women of his language who were positioned between two histories, and they only said it at that moment in the war for liberation, legitimized by the insurrectional movement. They said it then, each one said it, *my people, our people.*

As for me, separated since my first cries in the world, the irreducible split, I don't say *my people,* not to one side nor the other. Would I enjoy saying *my people,* as I have so often heard it in the language of exiles? Maybe, provided that I could say no, that I could write what I want, even if people perhaps think I'm betraying my father and *his people.*

∞

My father won't read this book, and I can write it because he won't read it. Perhaps he would've said: "My daughter, you write, that's good. I taught you to read, and you know how to read every book, that's good. It's as though you went to seek knowledge in China during the time of the Prophet. But you really didn't understand anything. It's too late."

GLOSSARY

abaya—full-length outer garment for women

chéchia—skullcap

chibani—designation for the now elderly first generation of Maghrebian immigrants to France

congaï—concubine

djebel—mountain

djellabah—long robe, piece of clothing with a hood

douar—group of dwellings, most often bringing together families claiming to be descendants of a common ancestor; village

Eid—Muslim holiday and feast marking the end of Ramadan

gandourah—traditional North African robe for men or women, usually made of silk or cotton, with an embroidered V-neck

haïk—women's traditional white veil

hammam—Moorish bath

hijeb—head covering for women

khôl—cosmetic used to darken the area around the eyes; antimony powder

koubba—dome; by extension the domed shrine of a *marabout* or holy man

le bon nègre—in eighteenth-century French fiction, an African slave who is "good" (enlightened); the master educates him in Western culture and values

madrasa—Islamic secondary school in which instruction is in Arabic

maquis—underground forces

marabout—important holy person of popular veneration; holy person's tomb; shrine honoring a person

muezzin—person who calls the faithful to prayer

mujahideen—in the context of the Algerian War, freedom fighters

pied-noir—Algerian-born French during the colonial period

GLOSSARY

Ramadan—religious fasting during the month of Ramadan (ninth
   month of the Muslim calendar)
Roumia—(originally "Roman") designation for a French (i.e.,
   Christian) woman or a foreign woman; other forms are Roumi
   (masculine) and Roumiette (feminine diminutive)
sans nom patronymique—literally "without a last name"
saroual—loose-fitting trousers
village nègre—African quarter of a town or city

AFTERWORD

Mildred Mortimer

A francophone writer of mixed French and Algerian origins, Leïla Sebbar is a prominent postcolonial writer of fiction and autobiographical narrative. Much of her fiction, particularly her early novels, has centered on the lives of Algerian immigrants in France, but other fictional works deal with the Algerian War, 1954–62, and Algeria's undeclared civil war in the 1990s. Although Sebbar first wrote fiction to re-create the world of Algerians living in Algeria and in France, she soon delved into personal narrative, probing her own memories of childhood and adolescence in colonial Algeria in an attempt to bring together conflicting elements of her dual heritage. This speleological endeavor has resulted in several autobiographical texts, including the present collection of personal essays, now in English translation.[1]

The origin of this collection of autobiographical essays can be traced back to an earlier publication. In early spring 1983, Leïla Sebbar and Nancy Huston, two young women writers living and working in Paris, began a correspondence that would express their sense of exile in France, the country where they had settled as young adults, studying, working, writing, and raising their families. Continuing for a year and a half, the exchange of letters explored various dimensions of exile as it confirmed a shared sense of finding a home in fiction. A series of thirty letters that alternate two voices, the correspondence was subsequently published as *Lettres parisiennes: Autopsie d'exil* in 1986.

AFTERWORD

In the epistolary exchange, Huston, an anglophone Canadian living in Paris, explained that she chose to write most of her work in French rather than in her native English. Sebbar, a Franco-Algerian born and raised in Algeria and residing in Paris as well, revealed that she had no such choice. Political and familial circumstances that she carefully analyzes in the various essays that make up *Arabic as a Secret Song* resulted in her acquiring French, her mother's language, the language of the colonizer, but not Arabic, her father's mother tongue, the language of the colonized.

Published after a series of novels that established Sebbar as a writer of Algerian immigrant life in France, the correspondence offered her the literary space in which to introduce and develop the autobiographical narrative. A collaborative work of nonfiction, it is significant not only for shedding light upon the struggle of exilic writers to find their place in the world but also because it encouraged the writer to express a personal and authentic self. For example, in one letter to Huston she writes, "And so for me, fiction is the suture that masks the wound, the distance between the two shores" (147), using an extended metaphor to explain that the two shores are separated not only by an extensive body of water but also by a divided history and that for her, fiction eases the pain of a fractured identity. She adds:

> I am there at the crossroads, serene at last, finally in my place, for I am a *croisée,* a hybrid in search of connection, writing within a lineage, one that is always the same. It is tied to history, to memory, to identity, to tradition, and to transmission, by which I mean the search for ascendants and descendants, seeking a place in the history of a family, a community, a people with regard to History and the universe. It is in fiction that I feel I am a free subject (free of mother, father, clan, dogma) and strengthened by the burden of exile. Only

there do I muster body and soul to span the two banks, both upstream and downstream . . . (147)

Thus, fiction writing allows the Franco-Algerian writer to "span the two banks," bringing her two divergent cultural worlds together. Her use of sea imagery, a clear reference to the Mediterranean Sea, which touches both French and Algerian shores, places her and her fictional protagonists within a Mediterranean geographical and cultural context.[2]

Despite the feeling of serenity expressed in this passage of *Lettres parisiennes,* anxiety enters Sebbar's letters, specifically with respect to her attempt to define herself to the public. Evoking the identity quest, a theme woven throughout the essays in the present volume, she acknowledges the inability to find a simple answer to Montaigne's question "Qui suis-je?" (Who am I?):

> Every time I have to give my identity before an unknown diverse public, I flounder. I find myself saying: It's complicated . . . it's a long story . . . I cannot answer so quickly. Or, I define myself in negative terms: I am not who you think I am, whom you are expecting or would like to see. In short, since we are dealing with my books and I am here as a writer and an individual, let me say: I am not an immigrant, nor a child of immigrants. I am not a North African writer of French expression. I am not of French stock. My mother tongue is not Arabic. (133)

She adds that some North Africans—individuals in transit, exiles, or immigrants—have taken her to task for depicting Arabs in her work upon learning that she does not speak Arabic. Their hostility reflects the view that her Arabic name misrepresents an identity that, in its complex relationship to Algeria and its culture, should not attempt to speak for Algerians at home or abroad, past or present. They refuse to admit that although she does not inhabit the cultural space of novelists such as Azouz Begag, Mehdi Charef, and, more recently, Mabrouk Rachedi, writers who grew up in France in the low-income housing projects they describe, she aptly portrays the culture of the immigrant *banlieue* in her texts, because she shares their sense of psychological dislocation and exile.

Compelled to find a definition of self that would make sense to her and her public, she comes up with the following: "I am French, a French writer who has a French mother and an Algerian father, and the characters in my books do not express my identity; they are the signs of my *histoire de croisée*, my history as a hybrid" (134).

As a cultural hybrid, the Franco-Algerian writer shares common ground with the late Palestinian American scholar and critic Edward Said: they are both positioned at the crossroads of East and West.[3] In his reflections on a life in exile, "The Mind of Winter," published in 1984, the year in which Sebbar and Huston explore the theme in their exchange of letters, Said carefully examines the meaning of the exilic experience, weighing the gains against the losses.[4] On the one hand, he defines exile negatively, in terms of pain: "Exile is the unbearable rift forced between a human being and a native place, between the self and its true home" (49). On the other hand, he posits plurality of vision as compensation, at least in part, for psychological dislocation: "Most people are principally aware of one culture, one setting, one home; exiles are aware of at least two, and this plurality of vision gives rise to an awareness of simultaneous dimensions, an awareness that—to borrow a phrase from music—is contrapuntal" (55). With the adaptation to a new environment, Said explains, the exile finds new customs, activities, and expressions that conflict with the memory of the old. These do not replace the others but result in contrapuntal juxtaposition. In the final analysis, the exile's new way of seeing, hearing, and experiencing a new and different environment provides an enriching experience, one that compensates for the loss of an earlier home with its familiar customs, activities, and social codes.

Thus, in contrast to the postcolonial theorist Homi Bhabha's view of the "third space" as a positive alternative to a fixed essentialized identity, Said is more cautious, factoring in the psychological dislocation that far too often accompanies physical displacement. It is this sense of psychological dislocation that is at the heart of the present volume, and indeed Sebbar's entire oeuvre, a corpus that spans several decades, embraces various writing styles, and includes several genres—novels, short stories, autobiographical narratives, essays. Returning to the metaphor of the suture, which Sebbar introduced in her letter to Huston—"fiction is the suture that masks the wound, the distance between the two shores"—I suggest that as we examine the essays in the present volume, we ask whether autobiographical narrative may be the suture that closes, rather than masks, the wound. If so, does autobiographical narrative, rather than fiction, best heal a fractured identity?

The Writer's Biography

Leïla Sebbar was born in Aflou, a small town in western Algeria, on November 9, 1941. Her father, Mohammed Sebbar, an Algerian schoolteacher, had met his wife, Renée Bordas, a Frenchwoman engaged in the same profession, while attending a seminar for teachers in Bordeaux.[5] She accompanied him back to Algeria, where, beginning in the early 1940s, the couple taught and raised their four children, both tasks becoming increasingly difficult once the Algerian War began in November 1954. The violent anticolonial struggle waged between the colonized population seeking independence from France and the French colonialists who opposed them would be trying for both communities, and certainly for mixed families, who were often

AFTERWORD

viewed with suspicion by both warring sides. Life in Algeria was particularly difficult for the Sebbar family when, in 1957, Mohammed Sebbar was arrested by French authorities and imprisoned for several months.

During Leïla's childhood years, the family moved several times, from Aflou to Hennaya, Blida, and then Algiers. In each place, the couple lived with their children within the school compound, in lodging provided by the Ministry of Education to her father, first a teacher, then principal of various French colonial schools that educated indigenous boys; her mother taught at the same schools. In her autobiographical writings, Sebbar suggests that this unique domestic space, a home situated in neither the French part of town nor the Arab section, but within the confines of the French colonial school, contributed to her sense of distance from both cultures. Indeed, the Sebbar family—mother, father, and the four children—inhabited a "third space," culturally and spatially separated from both the *piedsnoirs,* that is, the French settler population, and the *indigènes,* the Arab and Berber communities of colonial Algeria.

Completing her secondary-school education in Algeria, Leïla left for France in 1961 to obtain an undergraduate degree in French literature at the University of Aix-en-Provence. In 1963 she moved to Paris for graduate studies leading to a career as a high-school French teacher in Paris. Her doctoral dissertation, "Le mythe du bon nègre ou l'idéologie coloniale dans la production romanesque du XVIIIe siècle" (The myth of the *bon nègre,* or colonial ideology in eighteenth-century fiction), defended in 1974, reflects her commitment to examining the myth of the Other, foreshadowing her works of fiction.

During the turbulent period of social unrest in May 1968, Sebbar embraced the student and feminist movements. She subsequently wrote for several feminist revues, including *Sorcières* and *Histoires d'Elles,* a publication founded with Huston and other friends in 1976. From 1979 to 1981 she wrote for *Sans*

AFTERWORD

Frontières, a journal concerned with immigration issues, contributing a column, "Mémoires de l'immigration," which comprised interviews with immigrants in France. Her articles also appeared in well-known literary journals such as *Les Temps Modernes* and *La Quinzaine Littéraire*. And prior to the publication of her early novels, she published two sociological studies, *On tue les petites filles* (1978), which deals with the physical abuse of young girls, and *Le pédophile et la maman* (1980), a study of parental love and sexuality.

Sebbar's first novel, *Fatima ou les Algériennes au square* (Fatima or the Algerian women in the square), published in 1981, explores the psychological and cultural conflicts within a Maghrebian family in the working-class suburbs of Paris, conflicts that lead the young daughter to leave the family. *Shérazade, 17 ans, brune, frisée, les yeux verts (Sherazade: Missing, aged 17, dark curly hair, green eyes)*, published the following year, is the first novel of a trilogy that chronicles the adventures of Sherazade, also a daughter of Maghrebian immigrants who leaves home. Readers meet her living with an assorted group of runaways, all of whom live clandestinely, surviving by their wits and often engaging in crime—drugs, prostitution, robbery. This fiercely independent, rebellious young girl has appealed to young people on both sides of the Atlantic; the English translation of the novel appeared in 1991. Although the novelist, as previously noted, is not a member of the community she depicts, her experience of cultural crossing and exile, as well as her French nationality, encompassing unique origins, have to be seen as determining factors in her literary trajectory, enabling her, through her writings, to skillfully portray the Maghrebian immigrant experience in France.

Concurrently with her novels and short stories, Sebbar has edited collections of writers' recollections of childhood in the colonial world. Some, such as *Mes Algéries en France* (My Algerias in France) deal specifically with colonial Algeria. Others, including *Une enfance outremer* (A childhood overseas), include memories of childhood in Corsica, Tunisia, Egypt, and other Mediterranean spaces. These texts contextualize Sebbar's childhood experience within a larger geopolitical framework, contributing to her understanding of her own specific childhood and adolescence in colonial Algeria. Accompanied by personal photographs, which bring images to the process of historical memory, and drawings by her son, the artist Sébastien Pignon, these recollections—often collections of short personal essays by thirty or more contributors—form a fragmented, collective autobiography of a bygone era. In addition, she has provided text for images drawn from Algerian history, contributing to Jean-Michel Belorgey's collection of late-nineteenth-and early-twentieth-century postcards of North African women and to Marc Garanger's album of photographs of rural Algerian women, taken by the photographer in 1960. Thus, through her multifaceted literary output—fiction, nonfiction, individual and collective autobiography—she continues to be a very productive writer and an important voice in francophone literature today.

Arabic as a Secret Song: A Series of Reflections on Language and Culture

The nine essays that make up the present volume are, as the title suggests, an exploration of the writer's relationship to the Arabic language. Expressing the complexities of writing in French, her mother's tongue, while being separated from Arabic, her father's maternal language, Sebbar examines the complex issue of cultural domination in colonial Algeria as she articulates her struggle to live productively in the *entre-deux,* the space between two cultures.

The title, *Arabic as a Secret Song,* provides readers with several clues to the text. First, the Arabic language is a presence in the writer's world despite her lack of linguistic competency in this domain. Second, the language is linked to secrecy, to what is purposely concealed from view, as well as knowledge that is withheld. Yet, with secrecy comes exclusion: if some individuals—or communities—share a secret, others will be kept from it. In the Sebbar family, the father speaks Arabic, but his wife and children do not. Third, by linking the Arabic language to song, Sebbar introduces the universal themes of cultural transmission and memory. How many of us have memories of songs learned in childhood that were connected to a forgotten past? The title, therefore, defines Sebbar's relationship to a language that is part of her cultural heritage but one she never appropriated. Yet the Arabic language has become an indirect and constant referent in her world. Although she hears it distinctly but can neither decipher it nor use it as a means of self-expression, this linguistic trace has led her to embrace a culture that, even though she may not be able to grasp it in its entirety, she approaches with knowledge, respect, and sensitivity.

The earliest essay of the collection was published in 1978, and the most recent in 2006, with two previously unpublished essays dating from 2009 and 2010 included in the text as well. Thus, the text spans a period of several decades, in which the writer's thoughts and perceptions have evolved. Originally published separately in journals before being grouped together for this collection, they actually represent a two-stage process. *Arabic as a Secret Song* first appeared in 2007 as a collection of six essays. The collection was revised and reissued in 2010, with the additional essays providing new perspective on the writer's autobiographical project, her exploration of a fractured identity seeking reconciliation with the Self.

With the question of language at the heart of the nine essays, readers are compelled to ask, Why didn't Sebbar learn Arabic as a child growing up in colonial Algeria? Why does she feel this lack of linguistic competency so strongly as an adult? Does this lacuna in fact represent a larger issue, the difficulty, if not impossibility, of embracing a dual heritage when one is at war with the other? In other words, can the writer dwell more or less comfortably in the *entre-deux,* the third space, when, during her formative years, the two components of her identity were engaged in a violent anticolonial war? To grasp the dynamics within the Sebbar family that led the parents to make specific cultural and linguistic choices for themselves and their children, we must take into account the colonial structure erected by the French in Algeria, as well as the subsequent liberation struggle, examining the effects of both historical elements on communities, families, and individuals.

The Colonial Enterprise

Despite a proposed program of assimilation, the intent of the colonial power was to confiscate Algeria's fertile land for French settlers, thereby creating a *colonie de peuplement,* a settler colony. Thus, beginning with the conquest of 1830, French colonial rule created a significant gap between the colonized and the colonizer in the political, social, and economic spheres. In addition, the colonizer largely ignored or denigrated the language, traditions, and cultural production of the colonized.

In 1845 the overseas colony was divided into three separate regions—Algiers, Oran, and Constantine—each inhabited by an indigenous population as well as a European settler population that continued to grow throughout the following years. Two decades later, the *senatus-consulte* of 1865 subjected colonized Algerians to French laws but then denied them the rights of political citizenship. In 1870 the Crémieux laws granted citizenship to Algerian-born Jews, thus creating a wedge between the Muslim and Jewish communities in Algeria. In 1881 the Code de l'indigénat produced a list of offenses punishable in Algeria when committed by Muslims although not illegal according to French common law. These offenses included speaking discourteously to a French official and traveling in the country without a permit. It is not surprising that indigenous rebellions occurred throughout this era: Emir Abdelkader's armed resistance in the 1840s, the Kabyle insurrection of 1871. Yet these revolts proved unequal to French military power.[6]

Although indigenous military actions against the French subsequently ceased, the twentieth century saw a sustained political reaction to colonial injustice as Algerians faced further upheavals. World War I brought Algerians into the French army and French factories, replacing French workers who were at the front. In addition, impoverished Algerians found work as migrant laborers and as miners in France. Hence, poverty, land dispossession, unfavorable laws, and migration all contributed to a growing sentiment of alienation and discontent. An indigenous Arab and Berber population that numbered 9 million—in contrast to the 1 million European settlers who controlled a colony that was now administratively an integral part of France—chafed under minority rule.

Throughout the colonial period, the education of Algerian Muslims was purposely neglected. In contrast to the policy in Metropolitan France of promoting education as the path to social promotion, the *pied-noir* community saw to it that their own children, but not the indigenous populations, were educated. As the historian Tony Smith points out, the French of Algeria vetoed, diverted, and refused funds from Paris for the education of Arab and Berber children in a deliberate effort to keep Algerian Muslims out of the modern economic sector (93–94). When the Algerian War began in 1954, 86 percent of Algerian men and 95 percent of Algerian women were illiterate, a statistic the historian John Ruedy views as a "monumental indictment of a system that for more than a century had claimed to be civilizing the uncivilized" (126).

Imbued with the secular values of the Third Republic, the

writer's father, Mohammed Sebbar, devoted his professional life to educating the children of his compatriots. He and his French wife taught in schools reserved for indigenous children, but their own children, as French nationals, attended French schools. Both school systems gave children a French education, completely ignoring Arab and Berber linguistic, cultural, and historical references. Within his generation, Mohammed Sebbar and fellow Arab and Berber graduates of the École Normale de Bouzarea, the teacher-training school in Algiers, were rare exceptions to France's almost complete neglect of Algerian Muslim education. It was only after the Algerian War began that the French government changed its policy in a futile attempt to stem the tide of revolution and dissuade the colonized population from supporting the FLN (Front de Libération Nationale). Too little came too late.

The Algerian War

The anticolonial struggle began on November 1, 1954, when FLN guerrillas attacked military installations, police posts, communications facilities, and public utilities in various parts of the country.[7] The seven-year-war that followed was waged in the cities and the countryside by revolutionaries actively engaged in the armed struggle and their supporters, who carried out acts of resistance, sheltered rebels, and distributed arms, tracts, and supplies. On July 5, 1962, Algeria, led by the FLN and its military arm, the ALN (Armée de Libération Nationale), gained its independence. The French colonial era came to an end. The toll on the population had been enormous. Although the aggregate number of deaths is the subject of a grisly historical debate, Algerians claim the war cost a million Algerian lives (Ruedy 190). In addition, by the time the war ended, more than 3 million rural Algerians had been displaced from their homes.

Hundreds of villages had been razed, and fields, pastures, and forests had been destroyed.

As a newly independent nation, Algeria was faced with millions of impoverished, uprooted peasants poorly equipped to enter a new phase of their political existence. In addition, most *pieds-noirs* fled the country, many fearing reprisals at the hands of the Algerians. And, many *harkis,* Algerians who had collaborated with the French colonials, were killed in retribution by Algerians, with others relocated to camps in France that became ghettos for a population repatriated to a country that was foreign to them (Hamadou and Moumen 339). Thus, the summer of 1962, while exhilarating for those who had won the war—the FLN militants and their supporters—proved extremely difficult for those who had lost, and indeed for the entire nation. Exile and dislocation were experiences common to both the former colonizer and the former colonized.

During the war, Mohammed Sebbar, as previously mentioned, was imprisoned by the French army. Accused of belonging to a network that distributed medical supplies to the FLN, he was arrested in 1957 and held prisoner for several months, an incident his daughter recounts in *Je ne parle pas la langue de mon père* (I do not speak my father's language). Although neither he nor his wife was actively engaged in the resistance, some of their friends and colleagues were deeply involved.[8] Moreover, as the principal of a school for Arab children, he was indeed a potential target of colonial extremists. His friend and former classmate at the teacher-training school in Bouzarea, the Algerian writer and educator Mouloud Feraoun, was assassinated by an OAS (Organisation de l'Armée Secrète) death squad shortly before the end of the war. Feraoun had been attending a planning session for Algerian postcolonial education the day he and his colleagues were killed.

An adolescent in Algeria during most of the war, Sebbar

AFTERWORD

did not participate directly in the independence struggle, nor did her three siblings. Indeed, as a boarding student in secondary school in Blida and then Algiers, she considered school a sanctuary that offered protection from the war (*Mes Algéries en France,* 67). When the massacre of Algerians occurred in Paris on October 17, 1961, an event she recounts in *La Seine était rouge (The Seine Was Red),* she was a student in Aix-en-Provence, France, the university town where, she admits, she could finally live "without the fear of war, without surveillance, without protection."[9] However, the war crossed the Mediterranean one Sunday afternoon in October 1961. In Paris, police brutally attack Algerians participating in a peaceful demonstration against the curfew imposed upon them by the chief of police. She recalls the moment: "I am alone, reclusive, and seated in this armchair from which I don't stir. I am listening to the violent and memorable history that is taking place while I am seated there" ("La Seine était rouge" [1998], 96). Expressing the sentiment of distance from Paris, where the violence against Algerians was occurring, and Algiers, the war-torn city where her parents were living, she evokes feelings of solitude and anguish as she listens attentively to the radio announcing the demonstration.

Sebbar's subsequent quest for transparency with respect to a massacre the French government had effectively silenced for decades complements her quest to understand her father's silence concerning the war. He never discussed his prison experience, nor did he share his personal reflections on Algeria's independence struggle with her. Sebbar's mother kept her silence as well and, as her daughter recalls, never showed any fear during the tumultuous war years.[10] Clearly, Sebbar would like to have discussed with them their personal feelings regarding France's failed colonial policy, which, by a twist of fate combined with keen intellectual ability, had turned her father into a member of a small francophone elite but excluded most Muslim Algerians,

AFTERWORD

including his own parents and siblings. In her quest to unlock the secrets of occulted history, she finds similarities between personal and collective silence, her father's and that of the two nations, France and Algeria.

By engaging the theme of memory, Sebbar joins historians and writers for whom it is essential to probe the past in order to understand postcolonial Algerian society. Benjamin Stora, a leading historian of the Algerian War, contends that the state of amnesia surrounding the events of the war has harmed France and Algeria. In *La gangrène et l'oubli: La mémoire de la guerre d'Algérie* he labels repressed memories of the Algerian War a form of gangrene sapping the foundations of French society. He warns that neither communities nor individuals can "exist and define their identity in a state of amnesia" (319).[11]

Significantly, Sebbar's quests for clarity and understanding in both realms occur decades after the events. Physical and psychological distance characterizes her relationship to Algeria during the Algerian War, the period of her adolescence and undergraduate university years. As she explains, the sociopolitical events of May 1968 in France, including the women's movement, were the catalysts for her psychological journey through memory back to Algeria (55). Only after a significant amount of time has lapsed, does she return to her Algerian past, writing in the French language and in France, using memory, as the critic Helen Vassallo aptly notes, "as a conduit to layer the two" (94).

Defining the Self

With the choice of her first essay in this volume, "If I Speak My Mother's Language . . . ," Sebbar thrusts the reader into a psychological dilemma, a crisis of identity. In childhood, as she recalls vividly, she comes to understand who she is not, rather than who she is: not a boy, not really Muslim, not truly French.

AFTERWORD

In other words, to the exterior world her identity is problematic. Yet in her family home her hybrid identity is understood and shared. This is the domain where her mother/teacher envelops the children in her language, French, and where the child finds refuge in the world of books.

It may surprise readers that in the first two essays, Sebbar recounts incidents of being verbally aggressed as a child by the Arab boys in the streets: they shout obscenities at the three little girls, daughters of the French schoolteacher, walking together to "their" French school. At school, she is not taunted or jeered; however, her classmates—daughters of colonial administrators, *pied-noir* landowners, European businessmen and shopkeepers—question her repeatedly about the differences that set her apart from them. As a child with an Arabic name and a Muslim father, does she belong to their community? Taunted as a French colonial by the colonized, held in suspicion for her Arabic "traces" by the colonizer, she finds refuge—her "third space"—by retreating into books that offer escape to foreign lands. In this regard, she writes of "insect's armor" protecting her complex identity (31). Although Sebbar clearly experienced the tensions and sharp divisions between the European and indigenous communities as a child, it was the war, she explains, that informed her that she was indeed a divided soul.

In the first four essays, the writer probes two points of conflict that shaped her childhood: first, her initial hostility toward Arabic, the language of the largely poor, illiterate, rowdy boys in the streets; then, her ambivalence toward a mother who carries out her role as strict schoolteacher at home as well as at school. Intent upon creating a "little France" within her home, and training her children to be obedient, well-mannered French children, Renée Bordas Sebbar shows no interest in Arabic culture, language, or customs. Her daughters master the skills their mother requires of them, but Leïla will subvert a key element of the educational project. An avid reader, she devours books written by and about rebellious, adventurous women and then chooses indigenous women as the female protagonists of her works of fiction. It is in this spirit that she creates Sherazade, the unconventional adolescent of the Paris *banlieue.*

As Sebbar charts her autobiographical journey, she always returns to the father(land) in her attempts to define herself (Vassallo 94). It is not surprising, therefore, that the original text, published in 2007, opens with the second essay, "If I Do Not Speak My Father's Language . . . ," which focuses upon her relationship to her father. The revised text, however, begins with the essay "If I Speak My Mother's Language . . ." (not published in the earlier work), which probes Sebbar's relationship to her mother. Hence, a significant shift in emphasis takes place in the composition of the revised text. On the one hand, this transformation reminds readers that the organic process of constructing a whole from a collection of individual essays may move the emphasis one way or another, particularly when the work is revised and expanded. On the other hand, it emphasizes the self-reflexive nature of the autobiographical project. Sebbar is perhaps more keenly aware now than before of the crucial roles both parents played in the construction of her identity, revising the composition of her text to reflect this new perspective.

If her mother's portrait is ambivalent, her father's is enigmatic. Refusing to break the silence surrounding specific events, key choices, and personal reflections that shaped his life, he complicates his daughter's quest for knowledge and clarity. As her text moves from her childhood memories toward an exploration of her personal sense of exile, Sebbar depicts a father who, although bicultural and bilingual, leaves Arab culture, traditions, and the Arabic language at the door when he enters the classroom and again when he returns home. Yet he speaks

AFTERWORD

the Arabic language with others—his mother and sisters, his Algerian male friends, his servants, the parents of his pupils, and people on the street.

Through his silence at home, her father transforms Arabic into a "secret song." His daughter can appreciate the musicality of the language, embrace its sounds and intonation emotionally, but she is unable to decipher the meaning of its words. Ironically, because of linguistic and cultural lacunae, the protective environment of the home cannot extend to public space. The children of this hybrid family cannot function biculturally in Algeria the way their father does, because he has not transmitted the tools that would allow them to grasp the culture and traditions of the colonized. Sebbar writes: My father doesn't speak to us in his language. He doesn't tell us about his people's legends, or about Djha, the sly little man who mocks the powerful and the despotic. Not a single book, not a single word in his language is to be found in the library (44).

An enigmatic personality to his daughter, the father is also a frustrating one, keeping his silence about a war she experienced in her youth and is trying to come to terms with as a mature adult. In addition, he and his wife, faithful to the secular values of France's Third Republic, keep religion out of the home. Neither the father's Muslim upbringing nor the mother's Catholic background enter the life of the family, creating yet another realm of silence (30). Thus, multiple gaps in communication occur, contributing, in Sebbar's view, to her sense of exile in both France and Algeria. Yet this unique relationship to Algeria has made her a writer of exile, and of the immigrant experience.[12] Plurality of vision, as Said reminds us in "The Mind of Winter," compensates, at least in part, for psychological dislocation.

Hence, the father's silence, which at first created a kind of amnesia on Sebbar's part, ultimately results in the daughter's profusion of words as she begins her quest to recover traces of his maternal language, Arabic, in France:

> To come back to myself, to say "I," I had to walk a long way, to talk and live at a distance at once real and close to the imaginary, I had to hear, far from the native land, everywhere where it was spoken, the voice of my father's language, the Arab voice, the foreign language, the intimate foreigner. In plazas, in parks and gardens, in town squares, under the plane trees, on benches, at the foot of war memorials. In the Arab cafés in Barbès, Montreuil, Belleville . . . (58)

At the end of a long process of questioning, Sebbar is able to reinterpret her father's silence. If she first wondered whether he had been consciously complicit with the model of France's "civilizing mission," a colonial policy that purports to instill French culture into the hearts and minds of the native population but rejects, ignores, and neglects non-Western cultures in the belief that they are inferior, she no longer does. After long and serious reflection, Sebbar is convinced that her father, a partisan of the Algerian independence struggle, used silence as a means of resistance against the colonial power, not complicity with it. In her view, it allowed him to remain faithful to his people, preserving a space, both linguistic and cultural, for him and for them. What his children may have experienced as a lack of transmission was then his way of setting his culture apart from Western influence. This space, however, excludes his French wife and his Franco-Algerian children. The children would never be French in the same way their mother was, nor would they be Algerian in the way their father was. Their self-definition and their destiny were elsewhere. For Leïla Sebbar, they were in the world of letters, fiction, and autobiographical narrative.

Returning to the question posed at the beginning of this

AFTERWORD

afterword—does autobiographical narrative rather than fiction best heal a fractured identity?—we can only answer by comparing the writer's fiction with her autobiographical narratives, which is beyond the limits of this essay. Anglophone readers should note, however, that to date, three of Sebbar's novels have appeared in English: *Sherazade: Missing, aged 17, dark curly hair, green eyes; Silence on the Shores; The Seine was Red.* Skyler Artes's translation offers autobiographical narrative to the selection of Sebbar's texts available in English. It is hoped that it will encourage readers to explore the writer's other works, including her fiction, for as the critic Michael Seidel aptly notes: "For the exile, native territory is the product of heightened and sharpened memory, and imagination is, indeed, a special homecoming" (xi).

In conclusion, autobiographical reflections may not conclusively heal a fractured identity, but they do add important elements that allow the exiled writer to transform rupture into connection, and the reader to grasp the complexity of the task. Leïla Sebbar, the "hybrid in search of connection," finds her home in the world of letters, and in so doing, she provides her readers with a rich corpus of literary texts.

Notes

1. See also *Je ne parle pas la langue de mon père* (2003) and *Mes Algéries en France* (2004).

2. The sea imagery anticipates a later novel, *Le silence des rives* (1994), which depicts the last day in the life of an Algerian immigrant in France who, as death draws near, returns through memory to the other shore, the Algeria of his youth.

3. Sebbar and Said offer similar perspectives on Orientalism, a concept both view as a projection of the Westerner's fantasy, the colonial myth of the Other. See Said's reflections on Orientalism in his study *Orientalism* (1978) and Sebbar's depiction of Julien, the young Frenchman obsessed with Sherazade, the young girl he pursues as an exotic object, in Sebbar's novel *Shérazade, 17 ans, brune, frisée, les yeux verts.*

AFTERWORD

4. Said's "The Mind in Winter" was republished in 2000 in a slightly modified version as "Reflections on Exile."

5. It is important to note that the fathers of two other prominent Algerian women writers were teachers: Tahar Imalayen (Assia Djebar) and Yacoub Benameur (Maïssa Bey). Significantly, all three women writers have evoked their father's influence upon their development as writers. See Djebar, *Fantasia: An Algerian Cavalcade,* and Bey, "Fragments" and "Mon père, ce rebelle," in addition to Sebbar's autobiographical texts.

6. For a detailed study of the policy of assimilation, see Haddour.

7. For a detailed history of the Algerian War in English, see Horne; and Ruedy.

8. In *Mes Algéries en France,* Sebbar speaks of her parents' friendship with the militants Djilali and Jacqueline Guerroudj, who were sentenced to death as terrorists and pardoned at the end of the war. Jacqueline Guerroudj's daughter, the historian Djamila Amrane, joined the FLN and was captured and imprisoned at the age of 17. Thus, her experience of the Algerian War was very different from Sebbar's.

9. Leïla Sebbar to Mildred Mortimer, 27 May 2007.

10. Leïla Sebbar, interview by Mildred Mortimer, 26 May 2014.

11. See Stora for a detailed analysis of this occulted history.

12. For a study of Sebbar's work that argues that she represents a unique position that does not allow us to classify her as a French, Algerian, or Maghrebian immigrant writer, see Karzazi.

BIBLIOGRAPHY

Bey, Maïssa. "Fragments." In *Mon père*, edited by Leïla Sebbar, 65–74.
Montpellier: Éditions Chèvrefeuille Étoilée, 2007.
———. "Mon père ce rebelle." In *A Contre-silence*, 80–90. Grigny:
Éditions Paroles d'Aube, 1998. Translated by Suzanne Ruta as "My
Father, The Rebel," *World Literature Today*, November 2007, 27–30.
Bhabha, Homi. *The Location of Culture*. London: Routledge, 1995.
Djebar, Assia. *Fantasia: An Algerian Cavalcade*. Translated by Dorothy S.
Blair. London: Quartet Books, 1985.
———. *L'amour, la fantasia*. Paris: Jean Lattès, 1985.
Haddour, Azzedine. *Colonial Myths: History and Narrative*. Manchester:
Manchester University Press, 2000.
Hamoumou, Mohand, and Abderahmen Moumen. "L'histoire des harkis et
français musulmans: La fin d'un tabou?" In *La guerre d'Algérie 1954–
2004: La fin de l'amnésie*, edited by Benjamin Stora and Mohammed
Harbi, 317–44. Paris: Robert Laffont, 2004.
Horne, Alistair. *A Savage War of Peace: Algeria 1954–1962*. 1977.
Reprint, Harmondsworth, UK: Penguin, 1985.
Karzazi, Wafae. "La réception critique de l'oeuvre de Leïla Sebbar."
In *Femmes en francophonie: Écritures et lectures du féminin dans
les littératures francophones*, edited by Isaac Bazié and Françoise
Naudillon, 67–89. Montréal: Mémoires d'encrier, 2013.
Ruedy, John. *Modern Algeria: The Origins and Development of a Nation*.
Bloomington: Indiana University Press, 1992.
Said, Edward. "The Mind of Winter." *Harper's Magazine*, September
1984, 49–55. Reprinted in a modified version as "Reflections on Exile,"
in *Reflections on Exile, and Other Essays*, 173–86. Cambridge, MA:
Harvard University Press, 2000.
———. *Orientalism*. New York: Random House, 1978.
Sebbar, Leïla. *Fatima ou les Algériennes au square*. Paris: Stock, 1981.
———. *Je ne parle pas la langue de mon père*. Paris: Julliard, 2003.
———. "La langue de l'exil." *La Quinzaine Littéraire* 436 (1985): 8–10.
———. *L'arabe comme un chant secret*. Rev. ed. Paris: Bleu autour, 2010.

BIBLIOGRAPHY

———. "La Seine était rouge." *Actualité de l'Émigration* 207 (1987): 14–16. Reprinted in *Le Maghreb Littéraire* 2, no. 3 (1998): 95–98.

———. *La Seine était rouge.* 1999. Reprint, Paris: Thierry Magnier, 2003. Translated by Mildred Mortimer as *The Seine Was Red* (Bloomington: Indiana University Press, 2008).

———. *Le pédophile et la maman.* Paris: Stock, 1980.

———. *Le silence des rives.* Paris: Stock, 1993. Translated by Mildred Mortimer as *Silence on the Shores* (Lincoln: University of Nebraska Press, 2000).

———. *Mes Algéries en France.* Paris: Bleu autour, 2004.

———. *On tue les petites filles.* Paris: Stock, 1978.

———. *Shérazade, 17 ans, brune, frisée, les yeux verts.* Paris: Stock, 1982. Translated by Dorothy S. Blair as *Sherazade: Missing, aged 17, dark curly hair, green eyes.* 1991. Reprint, London: Quartet Books, 1999.

———. *Une enfance outremer.* Paris: Seuil, 2001.

Sebbar, Leïla, and Jean-Michel Belorgey. *Femmes d'Afrique du Nord: Cartes postales (1885–1930).* Paris: Bleu autour, 2002.

Sebbar, Leïla, and Marc Garanger. *Femmes des Hauts-Plateaux, Algérie 1960.* Paris: La Boîte à Documents, 1990.

Sebbar, Leïla, and Nancy Huston. *Lettres parisiennes: Autopsie d'exil.* Paris: Bernard Barrault, 1986.

Sebbar-Pignon, Leïla. "Le mythe du bon nègre ou l'idéologie coloniale dans la production romanesque du XVIIIe siècle." *Les Temps Modernes* 336 (July 1974) 2349–75; 337–38 (August–September 1974): 2588–613.

Seidel, Michael. *Exile and the Narrative Imagination.* New Haven, CT: Yale University Press, 1986.

Smith, Tony. *The French Stake in Algeria, 1945–1962.* Ithaca, NY: Cornell University Press, 1978.

Stora, Benjamin. *La gangrène et l'oubli: La mémoire de la guerre d'Algérie.* Paris: La Découverte, 1991.

Vassallo, Helen. *The Body Besieged: The Embodiment of Historical Memory in Nina Bouraoui and Leïla Sebbar.* Lanham, MD: Lexington Books, 2012.

The texts assembled in this work have been previously published in collected works and journals:

"If I Speak My Mother's Language . . .": "Si je parle la langue de ma mère." *Les Temps Moderne* 379 (February 1978).

"If I Do Not Speak My Father's Language . . .": "Si je ne parle pas la langue de mon père." In *Voies de pères, voix des filles: Quinze femmes écrivains parlent de leurs pères,* edited by Adine Sagalyn, 153–64. Paris: Maren Sell, 1988.

"My Father's Body in My Mother's Language": "Le corps de mon père dans la langue de ma mère." In "Paradoxes du feminin en Islam," *Cahiers Intersignes* 22 (Spring 1991).

"The Mothers of My Father's People in My Mother's Language": "Les mères du peuple de mon père dans la langue de ma mère." In *Être femme au Maghreb et en Méditerranée: Du mythe à la réalité,* edited by Andrée Dore-Audibert and Souad Khodja, 159–65. Paris: Karthala, 1998.

"The Silence of My Father's Language, Arabic": "Le silence de la langue de mon père, l'arabe." In *L'Algérie à plus d'une langue,* edited by Mireille Calle-Gruber, 119–23. Quebec: Université Laval, 2001. Translated by Isabelle de Courtivron and Susan Slyomovics as "Arabic: The Silenced Father Tongue," in *Lives in Translation: Bilingual Writers on Identity and Creativity,* edited by Isabelle de Courtivron, 101–9. New York: Palgrave Macmillan, 2003.

"The Return of the Absent One": "Le retour de l'absente." In *Algérie: Littérature et arts; Mohammed Dib, Europe,* 240–48. Paris: Paris Bibliothèques Éditions, 2003.

"To Hear Arabic as a Sacred Song": "Entendre l'arabe comme un chant sacré." (Originally entitled "Énigmes.") In *Aux limites du sujet,* edited by Patrick Chemla, 85–88. Reims: La Criée; Toulouse: Érès, 2006.

"I Write of Arabic, Foreign at Home, and of God, Foreign at Home": "J'écris la langue arabe étrangère dans la maison, Dieu étranger dans la maison." Unpublished manuscript, fall 2009.

"I Write the Imaginary Arab, My Father": "J'écris l'Arabe imaginaire, mon père." Unpublished manuscript, January 2010.